Beyond Time

Book 2
of the Highland Secret Series

By
Elizabeth Marshall

In the writing of this book the author seeks to tell a story of fantasy, mystery and intrigue. To tell the story, it has been necessary to include some real places, historical facts and political bias. However, this book is written for entertainment only and the use of real places, historical facts and political bias does not reflect reality, the author's personal or political opinion, nor is it written to influence the reader in any way.

This book is a work of fiction. Names and characters are the product of the author's imagination. Any resemblance to actual persons, either living or dead, is entirely coincidental.

The right of Deborah-Ann Brown to be identified as the author of this work has been asserted by her in accordance with the Copyright, Designs and Patents Act of 1988.

First Published 2012

ISBN-10: 1478285052
ISBN-13: 978-1478285052

DEDICATION

I dedicate this story with all my love to my precious family, Andy, Sean, Kel, Ste, Rose, Dave, Caroline, George, Emma, Gerard and Lucy - a reminder of the many exciting adventures we have had over the years.

******

ACKNOWLEDGMENTS

Andy, I would not have written anything without you beside me. You are my world and I love you with all my heart! For all the wonderful times we have snuck away to York together, and the adventures that planted the seed of this plot, I thank you my love. For all the precious memories we have created together in York over the years
– you put magic back into my life.

Sean, where would I be without you? You have given up yet another summer for me. Love you so much big lad and thank you for everything you have done.

Kel and Ste, for your love and support, I thank you with all my heart. How you two put up with me, I will never know? You have stood by me and made this happen. I love you both so much, thank you.

Dave, Caroline, George, Emma, Gerard and Lucy – what a support team. I couldn't do any of this without you. Love you all and thank you.

Noreen Muller and Kim Bennett for being brave enough and kind enough to test drive this plot on its first draft. You are both absolute stars, thank you, so very much.

I've said this before and I'll say it again -
To the best public house in York, 'Ye Olde Starre Inne', you are absolutely, one hundred percent, responsible for my passion for ancient pubs, which is of course why I have chosen to use 'Ye Olde Starre Inne' as a key location in the 'Highland Secret Series'. Thank you for putting up with my endless questions and for providing the perfect retreat from a hard day's writing. Here's to Friday nights and your wonderful pub.

******

FOREWORD

HAUNTED YORK

Sit back, relax and prepare yourself to meet some famous residents of York – the most haunted city in Britain.

The dark streets are overcrowded, noisy and foul smelling. The air is heavy and wet. The smell of rancid waste fills your nostrils and hits the back of your throat. Lowering your eyes to the ground, anxious to avoid stepping in the sludge of filth that carpets the street, you notice an old man stumble and fall heavily in front of you. His death is not your concern.

You turn and guide your horse off the main path of the street and onto the cobbled courtyard of a posting house. A stable lad is grooming a fine black stallion as you emerge into the yard.

"Any chance of a drink for my horse?" you ask, noticing a trough of water to the side of the yard. The lad nods in the direction of the trough.

It is 1680 and you are watering your horse at what is now known as 'Ye Olde Starre Inne' – York's oldest licensed public house.

The air around you fills with the desperate cries of wounded and dying men and the unmistakable smell of blood and death hangs in the air.

Fear grips your soul as the sound grows louder and closer – but there is no one there, except you… and the stable lad.

The lad shrugs, "Ignore it. It is naught but the cries from the surgeon's blade. Before my time, you know… back in '44, after Marston Moor. They brought their injured and dying here, used it as a bloody billet hospital and morgue. "It is said the landlord was none too happy, him being a Royalist and all. Don't suppose he had much choice, them Roundheads having taken the city from Charles. Mind, it wasn't long after that they took his head as well."

So, if you are ever in York, I dare you to take a wander up Stonegate. Look for the banner stretched across the street and take the entrance below. Go hear for yourself the cries of the dead as you lift your mug of ale and sup to King Charles and his head.

Not brave enough for the 'Ye Olde Starre Inne'? Well… why not try the 'Cock and Bottle'? Ladies be warned however, of a man wearing a richly embroidered coat and tight fitting breeches, with dashingly handsome features and long, black, wavy hair.

George Villiers, the second Duke of Buckingham, born in London in 1628, was a close friend of Charles the second. He was a womanizer with an extraordinary talent for charming pretty ladies into his bed. So infamous was his character and reputation that his way with the ladies and his downfall from parliament in 1673 was immortalized in the nursery rhyme 'Georgie Porgie':

> *'Georgie Porgie, Puddin' and Pie*
> *Kissed the girls and made them cry*
> *When the boys came out to play*
> *Georgie Porgie ran away.'*

It is believed that on his retirement George bought a house on Skeldergate in the vicinity of today's 'Cock and Bottle' public house.

Apparently Mr. Villiers is still there. His saucy ghost has been caught spying on young ladies in the shower, following them to the toilet and fondling and stroking pretty customers of the 'Cock and Bottle' pub.

Shall I continue?

OK, but we only have time for one more, so grab a cup of tea and enjoy this, my last haunted tale for now!

******

PROLOGUE

Grace stood on the platform and watched the train pull away. She rearranged her handbag, bending slightly to grab the handle of her suitcase. Ten thousand pounds, a wedding ring, a crystal pendant and a pathetic suitcase on wheels was all she had to show for fifteen years of marriage. Well, that and her beautiful daughter. Jenny was fifteen, she needed her mother, but Jack had terminated the bond between Jenny and her mother many years ago. He was an influential man, a minister of their local church but what most didn't know was that Jack was cruel, vindictive and jealous. Women loved him, parishioners loved him, Jenny loved him, Grace had loved him, once, but over the years he had sought to destroy that love.

Jack had left early that morning. A meeting in London required his attendance, missionary business, or so he said. More like *missionary position* than business. She felt sick just at the thought of him. He honestly believed she didn't know what he was up to. That was all part of the excitement for him, thinking that he was doing something she wasn't aware of. But this time she had confronted him, bravely calling his bluff. Jack had lost his temper putting his fist through a door, shouting and shaking as if on the verge of a fit and his face had burned as red as the hair on his head.

1

He had branded her mentally insane and irrational. Even her daughter believed she was deranged. How could she think any different? The child adored her father; he could do no wrong.

For years she had hoarded money. The odd ten pound note here and there, carefully tucked away. Two months ago she had found the courage to open a bank account in her own name. Now she had escaped his tyranny, she was free. Clutching her handbag she nervously scanned the platform.

With the knowledge that she wasn't going to starve any time soon, Grace made her way from the station and onto the busy streets of York. She had her freedom; all she had to do was figure out what to do with it.

******

CHAPTER 1

She lifted her hand to her cheek as the familiar sting of winter hit her face. An air of urgency and purpose had come over the city. The light began to dim and Grace realized that nightfall was fast approaching. Tiny flakes of snow drifted from a heavily laden sky. She fixed her eyes on the orange glow of a street light and watched the snow as it floated to the ground. A knot of fear and loneliness tightened in her stomach as she scanned a narrow street to the side of the Minster.

Solitude had become her sanctuary, but just at the moment, Grace's heart weighed heavily and her thoughts strayed to home. She wondered when her absence would be noticed or whether anyone would actually care. She doubted they would. Her own mother and father believed she was neurotic, spoilt and teetering on the edge of a fashionable nervous breakdown. Besides, they were in America enjoying what they deemed to be a well-earned retirement. Jenny thought her the devil itself and as for Jack, she was quite convinced the only thing he would miss was his verbal punch bag. Oh, and perhaps his housekeeper and cook, but he could hire one of those just as easily.

She understood all this, yet still she missed the familiarity of home. But she reminded herself, she was free and no amount of stomach churning and homesickness was going to drive her back to that man. Filling her lungs with much needed air, she headed for a door, above which hung a sign advertising 'The Cavalier Hotel'.

As with most buildings in the inner city of York, this modernized townhouse lay in the shadows of the Minster. In fact it stood rather dwarfed beside the Minster. It was comfortable, clean and not too expensive. Her room had a small en suite bathroom, a television, a double bed, a single free-standing wooden wardrobe and a small desk on which stood a kettle and two cups.

"This will do very nicely," she whispered to the generic, nameless portrait on the wall as she set her suitcase in the corner by the window. Turning to face the portrait, she studied it silently.

"Who were you?" she asked, addressing the portrait once more. "Your eyes tell me you were a kind man, but not one I would like to be on the wrong side of either. Well, I guess we are kinda stuck with each other, at least until I can find some real people to talk to. So, what do you say, shall we have a coffee?" Grace lifted the lid of the kettle and made her way into the en suite.

"How do you like your coffee?" she called to the portrait as she rinsed the kettle and filled it with clean water. "Always better to rinse these things out, you never know how long they have been left standing."

Returning the kettle to its base she flicked the switch.

"Sorry, I didn't catch what you said. Was that... " she stopped and stared at the portrait, "... you look like a black coffee type of man to me. So shall we call it black, no sugar? Of course you don't want sugar. You've probably never heard of sugar."

Shaken from her thoughts by the sound of boiling water, Grace reached for the switch and flicked it up.

"I really have got to get myself a life. What am I like? Standing here talking to a portrait and offering it coffee. Dear, dear, me... And you can stop looking at me," she said, addressing the picture again. "Those damn eyes of yours! They make me feel as though you are as curious about me as I am about you. Right, I'm not doing this; I'm really not talking to a damn picture."

First thing in the morning she planned to register with every employment agency in the city; to change her address with the bank and buy herself a new cell phone. Grace ran her fingers over the ridged buttons of her Blackberry. She had switched it off when she boarded the train, vowing never to use it again. The idea of dropping it in a bin at the station had crossed her mind. But then the thought that it may be found and used to trace her had made her slide it back into the pocket of her jeans.

Feeling lonely and lost she clutched the cell tightly to her chest. Her eyes closed and she saw her daughter's disapproving frown, the hatred etched in her eyes by her father. A single sob escaped her and she realized she was crying.

The sun hadn't risen when Grace finally gave up her bid for sleep. Her stomach growled as she pulled on her jeans, a timely reminder that she hadn't eaten in over twenty four hours. Grabbing her handbag, she quietly pulled the door to her room open and ventured into the hall.

The homely smell of freshly brewed coffee drifted past her as she pushed her way into McDonalds. A daily newspaper lay on one of the tables. She wondered if Jack would be reading his paper. When he was home it was one of his daily rituals to read the Daily Mail at breakfast.

He was a creature of habit, a man who could not function without the structure of repetition. At precisely half past six every morning he would seat himself at the long dining room table, unfold his newspaper and reach for a cup of coffee. At precisely quarter to seven, Grace would serve him two six minute boiled eggs with two slices of toast. At seven o'clock, Jack would rise from the table and make his way to the front door where he would collect his leather sling bag and car keys and would disappear through the front door. A shudder rippled through her as she pulled her eyes from the newspaper.

"Hello, can I get you something?" the boy behind the counter called.

"Oh, sorry... err... can I get a white coffee – two sugars – and a bacon roll, please?"

"Is that a meal?"

"A meal?" she asked confused.

"With a hash brown or without?" he sighed in irritation.

"Without, please?"

"Fine. Is that to eat in or take out?"

"Eat in, I think."

"Take a seat and I'll bring it over to you," he said, in a singsong voice that hid neither his boredom with his job or irritation at her.

Blowing gently over the top of the coffee cup, Grace scanned the tourist map she had found on her way out of the hotel. It was difficult to make out where the employment agents were by comparing the map to the phonebook addresses she'd taken from the hotel lobby, or indeed if there were any agencies in the city.

The map wasn't directed at single thirty-somethings looking for their first proper job and a new life. She picked at the roll, eventually dropping it back into the small brown paper bag in which it had come. The coffee she finished, before collecting her rubbish and disposing it in the purpose built waste bin next to her table.

'Time to face the big wide world', she whispered, buttoning her coat and braced herself for the cold morning air.

Nine o'clock on the dot, Grace found herself outside what looked to be a respectable little employment agent. A card in the window advertised a temporary administrative and reception role. The only skills required for the job were the ability to type and a nice telephone manner. Grace had no idea if she had a nice telephone manner or not, but she knew that typing wasn't going to be a problem. Fifteen years as a Vicar's wife and a typing course – funded by the Vicar himself – had trained her well in the use of a keyboard.

A woman in her early twenties, with masses of flaming red curls, bustled up to the door and hastily pushed a key into the lock. Grace followed her through the door and waited patiently whilst the woman pulled a chair out and sat down behind a desk.

"Sorry, to keep you waiting, been one of those mornings and we are a bit short staffed here at the moment. Now what can I do for you?"

"I was just enquiring about the job you have advertised in the window, the one looking for temporary administrator and receptionist."

"Do you have any qualifications?"

"Well, I have a degree in history and a certificate that says I can type."

"What was your last job?"

"I worked for fifteen years as a Vicar's wife. The role was mainly administrative and fronting up social events for the church."

"Right, when can you start?"

"Now?" Grace replied more in question than statement.

"Excellent! I'm Kate and you are?"

"Err... Grace, my name is Grace."

"Nice to know you, Grace, now see that desk over there? That is yours. The password to the laptop is 'happy'. Log on and you can get started. We can deal with the formalities later; right now I have a mass of clients and contractors waiting for contracts."

Grace made her way nervously toward the desk, pulling the chair slowly from under the polished wooden desk. She couldn't help but notice how out of place the laptop looked on the ancient piece of furniture or how low the desk appeared. As she sat in the chair and lifted her hands to the keyboard she smiled, realizing that for the first time ever she was sitting at a desk that felt comfortable.

As her fingers glided swiftly over the keys and her eyes stared at the sheet of paper to her right, she noticed her reflection in the shiny surface of the desk. Her eyes blurred as the shape began to cloud and the reflection became the face of the man in her portrait. Fighting to drag her eyes from the image she willed her mind back to the work she was supposed to be doing.

"What are you doing? This is silly, get out of my head," she whispered to the image.

"Grace, did you say something?"

"No, sorry Kate, I was just reading through this document, making sure I haven't missed anything."

"OK, just remember, I don't bite. If you need any help or don't understand something, just ask."

Grace nodded, feeling guilty for having lied to the lady, but she could hardly cough up to talking to herself, or worse still, talking to an imagined image of a dead person on her desk.

"Why don't we take a break, Grace? You're on the last contract now, so if you send them to print, I will sign them and get them ready to post. When you have finished that last one, why don't you go and make us both a coffee?"

With the coffee finished and envelopes filled, Kate hastily gathered up the post and started packing up her desk.

"Nine o'clock tomorrow suit you OK, Grace?"

"That would be wonderful, thank you, Kate."

"Right, well we can sort your contract and banking details then, if that's OK with you? I have to rush as I need to get these in the postbox before the last collection. I am so glad you came along when you did. Honestly, Grace, I couldn't have got through all this on my own today."

Grace nodded, logged off the laptop, grabbed her coat off the back of the chair and followed her boss to the door. Kate's mention of banking details had reminded her that she needed to get to a bank.

Hungry and in better spirits, Grace decided to celebrate her new job with a glass of wine and a meal in a quiet public house off Stonegate called 'Ye Olde Starre Inne'. It was still too early for the evening rush and too late to encounter the lunchtime revelers, so Grace largely had the pub to herself. Having ordered a baked potato with a side salad and a glass of wine, she made her way to a small room which was sectioned off from the rest of the pub.

Rich wooden panels adorned the walls and lavish stained glass filled the windows. It was obviously an old building but just how old Grace couldn't be sure.

She lifted her drink and mindlessly brought it to her lips, staring through a gap in the partitioning into the main body of the building. Holding the glass against her mouth she focused on the bar and watched as the staff prepared for the busy evening.

She started as the hazy outline of a figure appeared behind the bar. In a bold movement of authority he raised his arm and pointed toward the door. He stood tall and bold, his face tanned and framed by the fall of his long wavy hair. He was looking straight ahead. Then slowly he turned toward her. His eyes burned dangerously as they followed something across the room. Grace drew a sharp breath as their eyes locked. She stared as they softened and his brow narrowed across the high bridge of his nose. For several moments she held his look until the shadow of a frown creased his brow and his jaw tensed.

The glass slipped from her hand, shattering as it hit the surface of the table. She jumped up as the cold wine flowed onto the denim of her jeans. Panicked, she cast her head toward the bar but the man from the portrait had vanished.

The orange glow of the street lights illuminated the city as she made the short walk from Stonegate back to the hotel. She bustled her way through a group of tourists following a costumed ghost guide and wondered what inspired anyone to believe in ghosts.

Then again, she mused to herself, I've been seeing ghosts all day. But I think I might be going slightly mad. Perhaps Jack was right all along. I do need help.

Grace entered the small reception area of the hotel and noticed the outline of the elderly owner's face from behind a book.

"Hi," she called, making her way toward the desk. The old man lowered the book.

"A good day, Mrs. Evans?"

Grace nodded, "Yes, thank you, and you?"

"Can't complain."

"I noticed you're reading a copy of 'Bushfire'," she said, looking for a convenient way to strike up a conversation with the man. "I'm a bit of a sucker for a good crime thriller. Only don't tell anyone or you'll destroy my carefully honed reputation as a romantic dreamer," Grace said, with a smile.

"Your secret is safe with me, Mrs. Evans."

"Actually, I was hoping you could help me. I'm in room twenty three. There is a portrait on the wall. I was just wondering if you had any idea whose portrait it is."

"Robert Hamilton."

"Who was Robert Hamilton?"

"He used to own this here establishment back in the sixteen hundreds. He was a Cavalier and a loyal supporter of the Stuarts. After the restoration he was given a handsome pension and retired. He settled here in York and bought a post house off Stonegate and this inn."

"A post house off Stonegate?"

"Oh yes, it's still a pub, you know? Worth a pint or two – has a nice crowd most nights."

"I think I may already have had the pleasure."

"Are you alright, Mrs. Evans? You look a bit pale."

"Yes, I don't feel too well. I think I will just head up to my room."

Grace sat on the end of her bed, staring at the face of Robert Hamilton. She felt his eyes watching her, searching her for answers.

"You're dead, gone, do you hear me?" she whispered to the picture.

His brow was arched, just as it had been in the pub. Questions screamed from his face. His wide jaw appeared to tense and a muscle to the side of his high cheekbone twitched.

Grace covered her face with the palms of her hands and sighed deeply to calm her rising panic. She had to be losing her mind. This just couldn't be happening, not now, surely not.

In sleep she heard the echo of his voice whispering her name. Slowly it drew nearer and louder, until she knew for sure it was him. He stood facing her, legs slightly apart and arms loose by his side. His dark eyes shone in the light of the fire.

"You are beautiful," he said.

She stared at him, her eyes fixed on the broad expanse of his chest as he moved slowly toward her.

"Come here," he said, as his hands encircled her waist.

She felt the muscles in his arms ripple against her as she relaxed in his embrace. Her head rested heavily against his chest. The crackle of a fire was the only sound save for the racing of his heart in her ears.

Her mind swirled with a mixture of realities as she awoke and lay motionless in the bed. She stared up at the beamed ceiling. Had she noticed it before? She couldn't be certain but it had been there in her dream, the same beams, only lighter. The ceiling had been wooden too, but now it was covered with plasterboard and only the edges of the beams were visible. She moved her head to the side and looked at the walls. They were smoothly plastered, but in her dream they had been uneven, rough and whitewashed. The carpeted floor hadn't been there either. Just the bare boards with sweet smelling straw and lavender scattered over them. The glass of the windows was thick and blurred, not the crystal clear it was now. There had been a large curve-topped chest, a fireplace and above the fireplace hung the portrait. Her stomach cramped and a ghostly chill ran down her spine as she tried to make sense of it all.

Grace swung herself out of bed and ran to the desk, tapping furiously on the wall behind it. A hollow sound told her she had found what she was looking for. The fireplace in her dream was now covered over with plasterboard. Clutching the edge of the desk she met the eyes of Robert Hamilton.

"Whoever you are and whatever is going on, it's not funny at all and I want it to stop."

Once again Grace beat Kate to the door of their office. She had not wanted to hang around in the hotel room, so had followed her routine from the day before; McDonalds for coffee and a half eaten bacon roll, followed by a leisurely stroll through the quiet city streets to work.

"Morning Grace. So glad you came back. I was worried you might not after I left you in such a hurry yesterday. Sorry about that, slightly panicked by deadlines. Come on, let's get this door open and the kettle on. I'm freezing."

Grace followed her chatty boss into the warmth of the office and headed for her desk, first checking the polished surface for obscure reflections before opening the laptop.

"Grace your contract is on my desk. Do you want to fill it in whilst I make us a coffee."

"OK, thanks Kate, will do."

The questions were relatively straightforward. Having typed up a good dozen of them the day before, Grace had the contract completed and signed before Kate reappeared with the coffee.

"All done Kate," Grace said, taking the cup from her boss.

Kate lifted the document off the desk and smiled.

"That was quick! There are a mountain of these things still to type," she said, nodding in the direction of a neat pile of forms on the edge of the desk.

"No problem, I'll get on them right away," replied Grace, unsuccessfully attempting to stifle a yawn.

"Bad night?"

"Sorry. I'm not sleeping too well. It's just being in a new bed. Takes a bit of adjusting to."

"Where are you staying?" she asked, glancing down at the contract. "Oh my God, Grace you are never staying there? That place is haunted to hell and back. My friends and I won't even walk past it. No wonder you aren't sleeping. Have you seen him yet then?"

"Seen who?" asked Grace, feigning ignorance.

"The ghost! Robert Hamilton. He used to own the place sometime back in the days of Charles II. Didn't marry till he was in his forties. They say he haunts the house looking for his wife. Tell me you aren't in room twenty three?"

"Well, actually I am."

"Oh, you'll never get a moments peace in there. That was his room, you know, his and his wife's. It's the most haunted room in the whole house."

"He must have loved his wife very much then?" Grace replied hoping to extract as much information from Kate as she could.

"Hell yeah! He fought for Charles I, and then he followed the Prince to the continent. Lived like a pauper for years but still he remained loyal to the Stuarts. He met a woman here in York and fell hopelessly in love with her. It's such a romantic tale. Actually, that desk you are sitting at now was his.

Cost me an arm and a leg to buy but the story behind it was just so beautiful I couldn't resist. His wife was an academic, a bit of an odd sort, but Robert had that desk made for her so that she had somewhere to read and write. It turned up in the cellar of the hotel you are staying at. The current owners found a letter to a local carpenter commissioning the work. In it Robert stated it was to be of the finest quality with exact dimensions to ensure the absolute comfort of his dearest wife. I used it myself for a while but it just didn't suit me. Too low, it gave me backache."

Grace felt the panic rising inside her as her boss talked, seemingly without taking a breath.

"Kate, what happened to Robert and his wife?"

"Well, as far as I can make out they disappeared for a good many years, but they are both buried here in York."

"Did they have any children?"

"Not so far as anyone seems to know. There is a story about his wife delivering a baby shortly after they were married. Some say the child was snatched, others say it died. Thing is no one ever found a grave for it. There weren't any other children that we know of. I think his wife was a bit past it when they married. She wasn't a young bride, but then he wasn't a fledgling himself. The story goes that she was a widow but there don't seem to be any records of her life prior to her meeting Robert so perhaps she wasn't from York."

"So how come you know so much about this man?" Grace asked.

"Because since I started this business he has done nothing but haunt me."

"Haunt you? Are you serious?"

"Yes, of course I'm damn serious. He hangs around this office like a lovesick puppy. It's like he's watching the place, day in and day out. He stands where you are now, by that bloody desk, just staring at it. I would get shot of the thing if it hadn't cost me so much money. I've tried to find a buyer for it but no one is prepared to pay the price."

"So you believe in ghosts then?"

"Don't you?"

"Well no, not really. But I guess there is something odd about all this. Why do you think he keeps coming here?"

"I don't have the foggiest. It's like he can't let go of the damn desk. I just wish someone would take it off my hands, but I can't afford to lose the money on it. Tell you what, Grace, you should go and have a word with the landlord of the Olde Starre Inne off Stonegate. Hear what he has to say and then see if you still don't believe in ghosts."

Grace couldn't face the pub that night. All she wanted to do was go back to the hotel and sleep. Unwrapping the sandwich she had bought from a bakery she sank heavily onto the mattress of her bed and looked up at the portrait.

"Right, Mr. Hamilton, I now know that I am not the only one you torment. Pray tell me dear sir what it is you want, because tonight I intend to sleep."

The portrait didn't answer. She hadn't expected it to, only it had felt good to acknowledge out loud that she wasn't deranged. At least she figured that if she was, then a number of other people probably were too. It wasn't that she had totally come to terms with the idea of being haunted. It was more like she had accepted that whatever was going on was happening to other people as well. She wondered if there was any point in changing hotels or asking to be moved to another room. It was an option she had considered but somehow she wasn't frightened anymore and besides which she was growing rather fond of the face in the picture.

Having showered and climbed into bed, Grace attempted to read a few lines of her book, an historical romance, called 'Forever Amber'. She had fallen absolutely and utterly in love with the main characters. A dreamer by nature, Grace read to escape the harsh reality that had been her life with Jack. In books she could be whoever she wanted to be and go wherever she wanted to go. Fantasy, romance, thriller, it didn't much matter as long as it took her away from Jack. Her eyes shut and the book fell softly onto the bed.

Again her mind filled with swirling dreams of contorted reality. She could smell the sweet perfume of the lavender and the earthy tones of the straw. A fire crackled and popped as the burning heat caused moisture to bubble out of the wood. A fierce wind howled and rain pounded against the thick glass of the windows. A man moved to close the shutters against the storm. She could see his strong shoulders silhouetted in the dim light of the room.

A single candle stood on a small wooden table beside her bed, its flame casting a gentle glow on the whitewashed wall behind it. Grace hadn't needed light to know every taut and toned muscle on this man's body. He wore a loose cotton shirt, but she knew intimately what lay beneath. She rested her hand on her chest and sighed as tiny butterflies danced in her stomach. Her heart raced and her body ached for his touch and she was happy, happier than she had ever been.

As the hours passed and night became day, Grace's mind fought to cling on to the dream, but as the dawn broke the magic died and she awoke alone in the empty room.

******

CHAPTER 2

"There's a karaoke night on at the Olde Starre Inne tonight. You wanna come?"

"Kate, I would love to but I'm not much of a pub goer to be honest. It's never really been my scene."

"Don't be such a bore; you'll love it, besides it will give you a chance to talk to Harry about his ghost."

"Oh…OK, I'll come but I'm not talking to any guy about ghosts. If you want me to believe in this ghost, then fine, I believe you, but please can we just leave it at that?"

"What's got you so edgy? Yesterday you were all ears when I was talking about it, now you're as tight as a clam."

"It's nothing, Kate, really. I'm just not a big ghost fan. I was curious yesterday, that was all."

"OK, hun, consider the subject closed. But you will come with us tonight, won't you?"

"Yes, I'll come with you but be warned, I don't sing."

"You'll love it, let your hair down, and have a good laugh. Just don't pay too much attention to Lisa, she's having a bit of a tough time with her husband and she moans a lot, but the rest of them are usually good for a laugh. You'll love Rose. She's bringing a mate along too. Actually her mate's pregnant, not far from due. She's from Scotland, a real love."

"I'm looking forward to it," Grace lied.

Just at that moment, Grace couldn't really think of anything worse than spending an evening in a pub with a load of drunken women and a karaoke machine. Jack had never allowed her out on her own. He considered women that drank without their husbands to be the scourge of society, the root cause of all social problems and second only to the devil in their intentions. Grace's stomach churned at the thought of what she was about to do but reasoned that to decline Kate's offer would be rude and ungracious. Besides which, she couldn't help but feel some empathy for this girl, Lisa, and looked forward to meeting her.

"Kate, tell me about Lisa?"

"Why do you ask?"

"No reason really, only you mentioned her name earlier and I'd like to know something about your friends before I meet them."

"Well there's not much to tell. Lisa is older than the rest of us but she went to the same school. Her brother was actually in our year so we got to know her through him. She left school early, married a druggie and he knocks her around. She's got a teenager and a small kiddy and won't leave the brute because she doesn't think she can cope on her own."

"That is sad. Hasn't she got any family that could help her?"

"God no! Her mother kicked her out when she fell pregnant. Old fashioned Catholic family – you know the type. She hasn't spoken to them since they found out she was pregnant with her eldest."

"Can't one of her friends help her?"

"We've tried, Grace, honest we have, but she just won't listen. She's been with him since she was fifteen. If she hasn't left by now, she's never going to."

Kate shut up shop early and the two women parted company, agreeing to meet up again at seven o'clock on Stonegate. Grace had two things she needed to do before then. One was to find something appropriate to wear and the other was to buy a book.

Just short of a year before, Grace had stumbled upon a book called 'Caring For Eleanor'. It told the most difficult of all stories – the desperate struggle of a young woman to take control of her world after a lifetime of abuse. It was the author's words that had given Grace the courage and strength to leave Jack. She hoped that if Kate's friend could read this book, she may find some comfort in its words.

With purpose, Grace headed off toward the nearest bookshop. It didn't take her long to locate a copy of the story she was looking for and having asked the shop assistant to gift wrap the book, she set off in search of an outfit for the evening.

Having never been to a karaoke evening, Grace had no idea what would be considered suitable and eventually settled on a plain black dress, a new pair of tights, some court shoes, a pair of plain gold hoop earrings and some makeup. It had been years since she had bothered to wear makeup. Jack had disapproved of its use, complaining that women who wore it were little more than prostitutes. Grace hadn't agreed with her husband but it had been easier to just stop wearing it. At first she had struggled, aching inside to feel beautiful, but life had worn her down and eventually it hadn't mattered anymore. She was a vicar's wife, nobody was ever going to look at her and consider her pretty. But tonight, if she could remember how, she was going to feel beautiful.

A bubble of excitement rose in her stomach as she planned how she would do her hair and make-up and what the new dress would look like on her. Suddenly she realized that she was no longer dreading the evening and admitted, if only to herself, that she was actually quite looking forward to it. Passing an off-license, Grace ducked in and picked up a bottle of white wine, it was Friday evening after all.

Seven o'clock prompt, Grace stood on Stonegate, surveying the street for signs of Kate. She wasn't surprised to find that her boss was nowhere to be seen. One thing she had come to learn about Kate over the past few days was that accurate timekeeping wasn't her strongest trait.

The air was cold and Grace wished she had brought a coat. The night sky weighed heavily with a mass of clouds and she wondered how dark the city must have appeared before street lights were introduced.

She found herself staring at the orange glow of the light beside her. Her eyes blurred and she looked away, toward a shop window. It was filled with trinkets, obviously aimed at gullible tourists. She felt the brush of a coat as someone passed her and she instinctively turned toward them. Only his back was visible but he had the appearance of a costumed guide. Her eyes followed him as he made his way purposefully down the street, his long black coat flowing behind. There was something familiar about him but she couldn't quite decide what.

Suddenly, he stopped rigid in his tracks. He turned abruptly, his coat swirling around him. She gasped as their eyes locked in shocked silence. The soft curve of his mouth quirked in a gentle smile and she raised her hand toward him. He took a long measured step toward her, his eyes never leaving hers. Her heart pounded fiercely as he drew nearer and nearer. The city dimmed around them. She could almost touch him. His hand was raised toward hers. He was going to touch her, take her hand in his. He was so close she could feel the warmth of him in front of her. His lips smiled and whispered 'I love you' as she stretched her fingers to meet his hand...

"There you are Grace, what on earth are you doing?" Kate's interruption dashed the apparition from Grace's view, "You look like a street artist performing a love scene alone! Come on hun, the girls are waiting."

The sounds of the karaoke machine bellowed from the pub into the street as Grace and Kate approached their destination.

"It's very noisy."

"It's meant to be, just relax Grace and enjoy it."

She followed her boss into the main section of the pub, standing self-consciously next to Kate as introductions were made.

"Ladies, this is Grace. She is new to the city, so let's get her a drink, although judging by her behavior in the street I think she may already have had a glass or two too many."

The woman laughed and Grace felt her face flush red. She had already finished a glass of wine and perhaps what she saw on Stonegate was alcohol induced. Either way, she wasn't planning on discussing the matter with anyone.

"What you drinking then?"

"I'll get these," Grace offered.

"Right, well I'll come and give you a hand," offered Kate.

"I take it you know what everyone is drinking?"

"It's vodka and cokes all round, except for the lady with the bump, she's on the diet coke and whatever you're drinking," replied her boss.

"I'll have a white wine."

"Hey, Harry, come and say hello to my new friend."

A graying stout man turned toward Kate.

"Hello, Kate. You and your mates here for the karaoke?"

"We are. How are you, Harry?"

"Getting older but no wiser. Still here and ready to serve you though," he said, with a cheery smile.

Grace liked this man. There was a soft welcoming air about him and she felt as though he were the sort of person she could bare her soul to and not feel judged. By all accounts he seemed the perfect barman. She smiled at him as he held his hand out to shake hers.

"Nice to know you, Kate's new friend."

Kate laughed, "Sorry you two. Grace, this is Harry. Harry, this is Grace."

"Hi Harry, great to meet you. This is a nice place you have here."

"It does me."

"Harry, Grace wants to know about Robert Hamilton."

"Kate, I told you not to do that," Grace chastised her friend.

"Well you might as well listen to what Harry has to say. He's an expert, nothing he can't put you straight on."

"I'm sorry, Harry. Kate seems to think I have an interest in this ghost but I don't. I just happen to be staying in the Cavalier Hotel."

"You missed out the best bit, Grace. Go on tell him which room you're in."

"Oh Kate you are being silly. This ghost doesn't exist."

"You weren't saying that a few days ago when you couldn't get any sleep in there."

"No but that was because I was in a foreign city and a new bed. It always takes me time to adjust to new places and I've never been one to stray far from home."

"Ladies, I hate to interrupt you but can I get your order, please? There's a bit a queue building up behind you."

"Oh, I am so sorry," apologized Grace as she felt her face flush scarlet again.

"Danny, come and take over from me here," called Harry turning to face a younger man at the far end of the bar. "Grace what are you drinking?"

"May I have six vodka and cokes, a diet coke and a white wine please?"

"I take it the white wine is yours?"

"It is, but how did you know that?"

"Because Kate's lot always drink vodka and coke."

"I'm flattered, Harry. I had no idea you had noticed," Kate said, with a big beam on her face.

Harry laughed, picking up a linen towel off the bar and threw it playfully at Kate.

"Less of your cheek young lady or you'll not be getting these drinks tonight."

"You'd never dare, Harry. I'm too good a customer."

"I dare say you are, Kate my dear," he said, handing Grace a large glass of wine. "Danny will get your drinks. Grace and I are going out front to have a little chat. There's too much noise in here. I can't hear myself think."

"But I'm with Kate and her friends. It would be awfully rude to just leave them... " Grace protested.

"Oh don't be so silly, go with him, Grace. You'll love Harry's stories."

Grace doubted that most sincerely, but followed the pub owner to the door and out into the courtyard at the front of the pub.

"This used to be a stable yard, you know. The inn was a posting house, years ago."

Grace nodded politely but silently wished she were back in her hotel room with her book. He unzipped his fleece and handed it to her.

"Here, put this on. It's cold out here for a lady."

"I couldn't possibly. You will freeze."

"Take the coat, girl. I'm a tough old man. A bit of a breeze ain't gonna kill me."

Grace smiled and took the coat. "Thank you, I do feel cold."

He motioned to a chair, propped up against a small round table that was obviously meant for summer use, but Grace obliged.

"So where are you from?"

"A long way from here," Grace replied.

"Aww, I see. A lady of mystery," he said, smiling across the table at her. "Well I hope you enjoy your time in our ancient city."

"Oh, I will... I mean, I am. Thank you. It is wonderful here. York is the most beautiful place."

"That it is, Grace. But we do have our fair share of the unexplainable. I'm guessing you've been having a bit of trouble in that area or you wouldn't be sitting here with me now."

Graced stared at him, her mouth open in shock. How could he know what had been going on? Was this just one big conspiracy, a joke, played on a newcomer?

"No need to look so surprised, girl. I know the hotel you are at. Everyone who stays in room twenty three complains and wants to be moved. I am surprised you've lasted as long as you have. The hotel must have been fully booked. The owner doesn't usually use that room for guests."

Grace relaxed a little and reached for her glass on the table. She had been hasty and jumped to an irrational conclusion. She took a large sip of the wine and sighed as it slid down the back of her throat.

"Do you know much about this ghost then?" Grace asked, thinking that Harry was going to tell her what he knew whether she asked or not.

"A bit. Why, do you want me to tell you what I know?"

She hadn't expected that response and she took another large sip of her wine. This man knew people very well, but still, she liked him.

"I guess... I am asking you to tell me," Grace replied surprising herself. She hadn't wanted to discuss Robert Hamilton with anyone but Harry had got her attention and she was intrigued to know what he was going to say.

The side of his lips quirked and he smiled gently at her. "If you keep gulping that wine down you aren't gonna remember anything I tell you by the morning. Relax, it's OK. I'm not gonna scare you."

"Sorry, I guess I'm just finding all this a little creepy."

"I can't argue that it's not creepy but I've lived with it for so long now that it doesn't bother me much."

"Do you have problems with the ghost too then?"

"Do I ever! Drove me almost to insanity when I first took this place over, did Robert Hamilton. He owned the pub when it was a posting house back in the 1660s. It's like we live in the same place and run the pub but on different levels of time. Mostly it seems to work for us. But sometimes the lines blur and our times mix, and then for brief moments, he is here and the pub is his, and I am here and the pub is mine. I have come to terms with it better than he has. A nasty temper has Mr. Hamilton when he is riled. Fierce protector of this establishment, he is."

Grace could feel her hands shake with increasing nervousness as the aging man told his tale. It all sounded so plausible, yet her logical mind told her he was a fantasist and a dreamer with too much time on his hands. But what if he was right? What if all the different timelines existed around one continuous circle and everyone who had ever lived in this pub were here with them right now, just hidden by an invisible barrier? What if all past worlds had never actually passed but continued to exist around us and all each new generation did was to build upon the last one? Grace shuddered at the thought. No, she had drunk too much wine. It was time to get herself away from this nonsense.

"Harry, thank you for our lovely chat, but I am so tired and think that perhaps I have had a tiny bit too much wine. Will you let Kate know that I have gone back to the hotel, oh, and would you give this to her please? Just tell her it's for Lisa." Grace reached inside her bag and put the wrapped book on the table.

"Of course I will. Can I see you back to your hotel, Grace?"

"No... no... really, I will be fine. A bit of fresh air and a good night's sleep is all I need. Thanks again for a great chat, Harry. It is very nice to know you."

"And it is very nice to know you, young Grace. I hope you will come back and see me again. I have something I would like to show you."

There were no dreams for Grace that night, just deep and peaceful sleep and Saturday morning arrived with all the promise of a beautiful winter's day.

She chose to have her breakfast in a quaint little cafe, just around the corner from the hotel. The city was a bustle of weekend tourists and shoppers. Resolved to spend a quiet day alone, Grace headed away from the hustle and toward the art gallery. A water fountain stood in front of the building. Mesmerized by the jets of water, she sat down on a bench and just watched as people came and went around her. The Kings Manor House stood to the side of the art gallery and, fascinated by the building, she made her way slowly over to it.

How easy it would be to accept Harry's theory, she thought, as she studied the ancient brickwork. It was almost possible to feel the history oozing from the building. There was an almost magnetic tension around the place that held her transfixed. The whole city was much the same. Every square inch of the place was soaked in history: traumatic, violent and bloody history. If only these walls could talk, she thought.

The sun was setting by the time she found herself back in the inner city. Most of the weekend shoppers had left and the number of tourists was starting to dwindle. A peaceful calm settled around the Minster as Grace headed back to the hotel. She couldn't make up her mind whether to grab a sandwich and take it back to her room for dinner or make her way up to one of the pubs. She didn't much fancy the idea of bumping into Harry again. Despite the fact she liked him – he seemed a nice man with a very friendly way about him – she hadn't yet decided what to think about his theory. It all seemed too bizarre for words, yet when she thought about it there were some things that made sense. Logic told her it was all rubbish, just the ramblings of a lonely man. Yet he seemed so grounded, so sensible. Grace's mind swam with it all. The man in her dreams, the portrait, the man on Stonegate. If it weren't for Harry and Kate, Grace would have put it all down to neurosis. Jack had always maintained she was mad. She needed time, time to get her head straight and time to think. It had been a traumatic week, the most traumatic she had ever known, and now here she was trying to reason whether ghosts were real or imagined.

Having bought herself a sandwich filled with warm roast pork and apple sauce she found a bench in St Helen's Square, outside the Swarovski shop, and sat quietly reading and eating her dinner until the air became too cold and the light too dim to continue. Sliding her book neatly back into her bag, she headed home to her hotel room.

Flicking the switch on the kettle, she dropped two lumps of sugar, a spoon of coffee and two spoons of creamer into a cup. She could feel his eyes upon her as she made her coffee. But she refused to meet his look. Her resolve was firmly set. No more talking to portraits, no more confused dreams and definitely no more late night chats, with anyone or anything about ghosts.

Leaving the kettle to boil, Grace prepared for bed. She draped her fleecy pajamas over the warm radiator in the room and headed for the shower. She was tired and looked forward to snuggling into bed with her book. She had closed the book in St Helen's Square just as Amber, the heroine of the story, had discovered that she was pregnant. The young girl was desperately hoping that Bruce, the hero, would finally ask her to marry him. Grace hoped that Bruce would do the honorable thing, but she doubted he would. Nonetheless, she was looking forward to finding out what was to become of Amber and her baby.

The warm pajamas felt soft against her skin as she slid onto the cool cotton sheet and pulled the fluffy duvet up to her chin. I could do with a hot water bottle, she thought, shivering despite the warmth of the pajamas. She took a sip of the coffee and opened the book. Her eyes blurred and she rubbed them in an attempt to clear the haze.

Unable to focus on the words she closed the book. Setting it on the bedside table beside a picture of her daughter - pain suddenly tore at her heart. She longed so much to hold her child and to share the bond that a mother should have with her daughter. With trembling fingers she lifted the photograph to her lips, holding the image of her daughter firmly in her mind. The bright red hair, so much like her father, the curls that proved she was her mother's. Jack's slim build on her own short frame. The joining of two people in one little girl who meant more to her than life itself. "Keep safe my darling Jenny," she breathed so quietly that even her own ears missed the sound.

Her eyes strayed to the portrait in front of her.

"You wouldn't understand," she whispered to him as her eyes filled with tears and, tired of holding them back, she relented to their flow.

******

CHAPTER 3

She smelled the sweet smokiness of burning wood and heard the gentle crackle of flames in the distance of her dream. The room was in complete darkness but she knew he was there, beside her. She reached out to touch him and felt the curve of his shoulders. He turned and wrapped his arms around her, pulling her closer. Tiny bubbles bounced in the pit of her stomach as she nestled into him, her back curved against his chest, her body pressed against the entire length of him. He reached for her hand and enclosed his large palm over it. His lips brushed against her head lightly as he rested his cheek against the top of her head. Cocooned in his embrace, secure in his bed, her heart safe in his hands, she smiled into darkness.

"I love you Grace."

"I love you too," she whispered.

"Please don't leave me again," she cried as the dream slipped from her clutches and dawn crushed the magic of the night.

Her eyes flew open and she turned immediately to face the place beside her where he had been. A sick feeling grew inside her as she was reminded that she was alone. Of course she was alone. She lived alone. That had been her choice. Sitting up, her eyes once more filled with tears as she looked at the portrait.

"If you can't be with me, why are you doing this to me? Please, just go away and let me live my life."

Grace jumped as a cold blast of wind howled at the window. It slammed against the frame and then the window burst open as another icy blast blew in. Shivering, she slid out of bed and closed the latch on the window.

"Damn thing, you scared me half to death. How did you get open?"

Glancing down at the radiator below the window, she bent and turned the thermostat up. The room was cold and she had seen a forecast in yesterday's paper suggesting that the city was in for a severe cold spell.

A thin dressing gown lay on the end of the bed; hardly practical for winter use but had been all she could fit in her suitcase at the time. Wrapping it around her she made the decision to spend the day clothes shopping. She wasn't going to be much use to anyone if she caught her death of cold.

The memory of her dream filled her mind as she recalled the glorious warmth and happiness she had felt with the protective arms of Robert Hamilton around her.

"How beautiful it must be to feel loved," she whispered to the portrait. "You were a lucky man to have had real love in your life, and your wife was a lucky lady to have you."

Sliding the photograph of her daughter into her purse and her book into her bag she wandered out of the hotel and into the cold winter wind and small flakes of snow falling gently from a miserable grey sky.

Making the decision to buy some warm clothes had been a sensible one. It was still early and most of the shops hadn't yet opened so Grace went in search of some breakfast.

It was Sunday morning and wandering down Low Petergate, the sound of church bells drew her down an alley to the Thirteenth Century Holy Trinity churchyard. It seemed a morbid pastime but inscriptions on gravestones had always fascinated her. She wandered along the paths scanning the words on the stone slabs that marked the life and death of each body below.

Her mind toyed with Harry's theory. It was an odd one alright and she wondered why no one had ever come up with it before. Then again, she wasn't exactly schooled in all things ghostly, so it was perfectly possible the idea was a popular one amongst enthusiasts.

The words on the gravestone were faded and unclear but Grace was sure she had found it, what she had been subconsciously looking for – the headstone of Robert Hamilton. She could only make out the first two numbers of his year of death, 'seventeen'... but that was definitely his name. The birth date was as clear as the day it had been carved, 'In the year of Our Lord 1626'. A perfect match to what she already knew of him.

"You lived a long life, Mr. Hamilton," she said, scanning her eyes over the rest of the inscription.

"Here lies Robert Hamilton, beloved husband of... " Grace read it out loud but she stopped short as his wife's name was unclear. She crouched down to get a better look but time had erased the words from the stone. A pang of sadness for the lady who lay beside her husband knotted in the pit of her stomach. How very tragic it seemed that this couple should have found love in life only to have its memory worn away with the passing of time.

She ran her fingers gently over his name, wondering as she did what his life had been like. There was little doubt that he had loved his wife and she guessed that his wife must have loved him too. There was no denying it; Robert Hamilton had been a handsome man. The portrait in her room was testimony to that, but everything else she had been told about him was mostly conjecture. Yes, there were a few scant facts: that he had been a Cavalier, that he had been richly rewarded for his loyalty and that he had owned an inn and a post house in York. But what Grace really wanted to know was what the man was like. Not what sort of career he had.

She mulled the idea of going to see Harry over in her mind. Finally, she decided that it couldn't do any harm. Her enquiring mind had set itself on a path and it was unlikely to be easily swayed. The shopping, she concluded could wait despite the cold weather.

Rapping lightly on the large black door set in the twisted oak frame of the entrance to the pub, Grace wondered if anyone would be awake at this time of the morning. Her question was quickly answered when a creak announced that someone was pulling the door open. A knowing smile filled his face when he saw her.

"I thought you might come back, Grace. Come in girl, it's cold out there," he said, ushering her inside.

The unpleasant aroma of smoke and smoldering cinders from the fire mixed with the heady smell of stale alcohol greeted her as she followed Harry into the main section of the building. Dirty glasses and empty plates and beer bottles littered the bar. It looked for all the world as if Harry had just walked out and left his customers to it.

"Sorry about the mess. I don't usually bother clearing up on a Saturday night. Try and get into bed a bit earlier and sleep in on a Sunday."

"Oh, Harry, I am so sorry, I hope I haven't got you out of bed."

"Good gracious, no girl. I've been up a while."

"Can I give you a hand to clear this lot up?"

"No, I'll get to it later. Would you like a cup of coffee?"

"I'd love one, thanks, but if you tell me where everything is I'll make it," Grace offered.

"So, what brought you back then?" he asked.

"I found his grave and I was curious, I guess. I'd like to know more about him. You seem to know so much about his life, I thought you might be able to tell me a few things."

"Now that is an interesting concept. I hoped the same from you."

"You did?"

"Yes Grace, I did."

"What could I possibly tell you about Robert Hamilton? I've only just come across the man. You and Kate are the ones that seem to know all about him."

"Well you could start by telling me where you're from?"

"Harry I don't get you. One minute we're talking about a dead man and the next you're asking where I'm from."

"Strange, huh?" he replied with a shrug.

"You talk in riddles. I'm not going to even pretend to understand what you are going on about."

Grace followed him into the kitchen. Spotting two mugs in the sink she rinsed them and reached for a seemingly clean drying up cloth on the side of the counter.

"How do you like your coffee?"

"As it comes, coffee is coffee to me."

Grace smiled to herself. If someone had asked her a few minutes ago how Harry liked his coffee she would have guessed that he didn't much care. She had always thought you could tell a lot about a person by the coffee they drink.

"Harry, what do you know about Robert's wife?"

"Probably less than you do."

"So you don't know who she was then?"

"Oh, I know who she is alright."

"Well then I would say you know a whole lot more than I do about her."

"What do you want to know about Robert's wife then?"

"Well anything really. What her name was, how old she was when she married him, …that sort of thing."

"Grace, put your cup down. I have something to show you."

"That sounds very cryptic, Harry. What have you got?"

"It's a portrait of Robert and his wife."

"You're kidding. That's amazing. I'd love to see it. How on earth did you get hold of it?"

"It was here in the attic. I came across it about twenty years ago."

"Did you find anything else besides the portrait?"

"No, just the portrait."

"It's odd you didn't find anything else. I wonder why no one ever spotted it before?"

"Time will tell you, Grace, you'll work it out."

"Work what out, Harry?"

"All of it Grace. It took me many years to understand."

"But you do now?" asked Grace, her mind racing with excitement as the natural historian in her took over.

"Yes, I do."

"Can I see it? The portrait, I mean?"

"Of course," he said, solemnly. "It hangs in the hallway, just before the ladies toilets. I put it there so that it wouldn't be missed if the lady... err... oh, forget it, just come with me and I'll show it to you."

Grace followed him out of the kitchen and through the main section of the building. He swiped a half-finished bottle of whisky off the bar as they moved past it and on toward the hall.

It was a narrow dark space with uneven plastered walls but she could see the frame of the picture as they approached. An excited bubble grew in her stomach as the canvas came into view. It was him, Robert Hamilton, his eyes sparkling, a broad smile on his face and beside him... was his wife.

Grace's knees buckled and her legs gave way as the room swam around her. "It's alright, girl, I've got you," he whispered aching to end her pain.

Harry instinctively raised his right hand and made the sign of the cross praying as he did that his Jessie had been right. He, Harry Hamilton, had given up too much to fail at this stage because of a lack of faith. He had to see this through, no matter what the cost.

Limp in his arms, Grace tried to speak but her throat was too tight, her pulse raced and tiny beads of sweat formed on her face. Harry lowered her to the ground and sank down beside her on the carpeted floor of the hallway.

"You have got to be... kidding! Is... this... some sort of joke?" she stammered turning white faced to the man beside her.

"No, Grace, this isn't a joke. That portrait is as genuine as you and me. Have it checked out yourself, if you want. Any expert will tell you."

She was no expert but had seen her fair share of genuine seventeenth century portraits and Harry was right. This was either a damn good forgery or the real thing. She breathed deeply, trying to calm her rising panic. It didn't work. She shook fiercely, her head swam and the room around her swayed as she lifted her knees and dropped her head onto them. She felt him rest his hand gently on her shoulder.

"It's OK, Grace," he whispered reassuringly, "I'm here."

"Tell me, Harry, how did this happen?" she wailed hysterically.

"I don't... I'm sorry... I...don't know," he lied.

"You must know! You must!"

Terror clung to her soul as she stared at the portrait.

"How did you know, Harry?"

"How did I know what?"

"That his wife wasn't from his time?"

The ageing man lifted the bottle of whisky and spun the metal lid off the glass top. She could smell the heady fumes of liquor as he lifted the open bottle to his mouth.

"Look closely at the portrait, Grace. Look at her wrist."

She scanned the image, fighting the rising panic inside her.

"It's my watch," she whispered.

Harry put out his arm and dangled the bottle in front of her.

"Here, have some of this."

Grace shook her head, wrinkling her nose at the smell.

"I don't drink spirits."

"It's time you started then girl," he said, lifting the bottle to his mouth again and taking a large sip.

"Harry, I don't understand. How could I have come to be in this portrait?"

"That is the mystery we must solve."

"That portrait must be almost four hundred years old. That's not a mystery in my book. It's beyond possible."

He nodded, taking another sip from the bottle.

"Can't argue with you there, girl."

"What am I going to do, Harry?"

"Well you're not going to panic, for starters."

"How can I not panic? I'm sitting here on the floor of a pub, in a city I've only been in a week, looking at a portrait of me that was painted nearly four hundred years ago."

"I can't tell you how this painting came into being, but Grace, you can't deny its existence."

She reached out and took the bottle of whisky from him. She ran her fingers absently over the label on the glass.

"What if it's just a relative? That would make sense," she said, turning to face Harry with hopeful eyes. The elderly man shook his head.

"No, Grace."

"Why? It happens. Genetics are a funny thing. There are people whose looks can throw back hundreds of years."

"And the watch?"

"OK, so that is weird. Someone could have painted it on. It wouldn't be the first time a genuine painting has been tampered with."

"I found this twenty years ago. The watch was there then and no one has touched it since."

"Twenty years ago I didn't have this watch. I was only a young girl."

"But your future self four hundred years ago did."

Grace lifted the bottle to her mouth and took a tentative sip, gasping and coughing as the fiery liquid slipped down the back of her throat. Harry laughed and took the bottle from her.

"You were right, girl. Stick to wine," he said, helping himself to another swig from the bottle.

Grace smiled and rested her hand on Harry's knee.

"You have been a good friend to me, Harry."

"Careful, you'll have me blushing," he replied, patting her hand gently.

"Would you mind taking that portrait down?"

"I think that would be a good idea. Now that you are here, we don't want anyone else putting two and two together. Especially Kate. She has a bit of a fixation with your future husband."

"Don't call him that."

"Sorry. That was crass of me. But it's your fate and you will have to come to terms with it at some point."

"How am I supposed to reply to that? It's a ridiculous notion. No one travels in time. Einstein's theory of relativity? Can't be done, Harry, it can't be done."

"But what if he was wrong? What if neutrons could break the speed of light? Just because scientists haven't seen it done doesn't mean it hasn't been done."

"That would turn the world of physics on its head."

"It would, but you can't discount something's possibility just because it will upset school curriculums."

"I need a coffee," Grace said, pushing herself up from the floor. Harry nodded and spun the cap back onto the whisky bottle.

"Bad habit," he mumbled to himself as his stiff body rose to stand beside Grace.

"You OK, Harry?"

"I'm an old man. Sipping whisky at this time on a Sunday morning isn't a good way to start the day."

"Have you eaten anything yet?"

"Never have breakfast. Messes with my system."

Grace laughed, slipping her hand into his.

"And whisky doesn't?"

"Oh yes, whisky does but it's a far more pleasant way to mess up your system."

"Come on you, I'm gonna make us both something to eat. If you keep drinking that stuff on an empty stomach you'll never be fit to open this pub today."

Smiling to herself she set about clearing up the kitchen and making some toast. He was still a nice man, even if he had just scared the life out of her.

******

CHAPTER 4

Back in her room at the 'Cavalier Hotel', Grace stood at the window and stared out at the street below her. What had happened that morning in Harry's pub had frightened her beyond anything she could ever have imagined. She'd spent the rest of the day wandering idly round York hoping the cool air would clear her head but to no avail.

She turned and looked at the portrait of Robert Hamilton. A dark shadow appeared to have crossed his face. His lips looked thinner and the muscles of his wide jaw appeared to have tensed. None of this made any sense to Grace. She rubbed her forehead thoughtfully. Was she in the middle of some terrible nightmare? It all felt real enough.

She cast her mind back to the day she had arrived in York. Less than a week ago, she had stood on the platform at York station wondering what her new life would hold. Now she had a job, a comfortable hotel room and at least two new friends – both of whom believed in the ghost of Robert Hamilton. Did she believe in it? Grace still couldn't be sure. She had certainly grown to know the man, more intimately than she should, thanks in no small part to her recent dreams. In truth she was falling hopelessly in love with him. Real or imagined, Robert Hamilton was stealing her heart and there wasn't a damn thing Grace could do about it.

A sense of urgency fell over her as she went about her final preparations for bed and the next morning. She glanced curiously over at the portrait.

"Will you fill my dreams tonight, Mr. Hamilton?"

A tiny flutter of expectation ran through her but sanity prevailed and the feeling was quashed. The dreams were idyllic, beautiful and in them she felt loved and safe. But, she reminded herself, they were only dreams. Her emotions were still too raw, her heart too tender to meddle in this nonsense. This man was not real. He was dead. Grace had seen his grave and it was as real as the snow that fell outside her bedroom window.

Sleep beckoned but she refused to give in to it in case he should come to her again. She was desperate with the need for him but, in the same breath, was beyond terrified of him.

His presence once more filled the room as sleep claimed her mind. Dare she trust him? Her heart leapt at the thought. She sensed him behind her, moments before she felt his strong arms wrap around her waist. His chest was rising and falling against her back, his breath warm and soft against her ear. She gasped as pleasure rippled through her body at the feel of his touch.

"Why do you haunt me, Robert?" she whispered, to the darkness.

"You are the one that haunts my dreams."

"I'm frightened, Robert. I don't understand."

"No my love, nor do I."

She had to resist, had to stop this. She fought to end the dream. Her mind clawed to break free, pulling at a thin thread of light that broke through the darkness. But he held her, trembling against him until the light of dawn rose around them.

"You bloody man!" she shouted, lifting the pillow beside her and hurling it at the portrait. It missed and hit the wall, knocking the kettle off the desk as it bounced and fell to the floor. She swung out of bed and grabbed the kettle base that was now hanging from its cable in the wall. She lifted her eyes up to the portrait, feeling sure she had noticed a brief smile. "I swear Robert Hamilton, this isn't funny. I advise you to wipe that smile off your face now."

Defeated, she sank onto the bed, lifting her hands to rub at her forehead.

"What the hell am I going to do with you?" she said, staring into his dark eyes. She glanced at her watch. It was getting late and she needed to get ready for work.

Her day passed in a fairly ordinary fashion. Kate chatted incessantly about anything and everything, mercifully managing to avoid the subject of Robert Hamilton.

During one of her frenzied monologues, she invited Grace to her house for what she called a 'girlie night' and Grace accepted. She hadn't had much chance to get to know Kate's friends at the pub and she certainly wanted to get to know Lisa better. She couldn't remember the name of the pregnant lady but if she were honest there was something about her that Grace didn't like and she silently hoped Kate hadn't invited her tonight. It bothered her that she had taken a disliking to the lady. She couldn't even remember her name and had spoken little more than two words to the woman. Rose, she liked. Kate talked constantly about her and Grace understood the bond between the two girls. They had grown up together and when Kate's parents had been killed in a car crash when she was fourteen, Rose's mother had adopted the girl. Kate's parents had left her some money which was what had enabled her to start the recruitment agency and buy her house, but she had lived with Rose and her family until she was eighteen.

From what Grace could understand Kate had moved out when Rose's mother had gone missing presumed dead. Some sort of hiking or climbing accident up in Scotland. It was sometimes difficult to follow everything Kate said. She talked incessantly and at times Grace wondered if the girl actually breathed through her ears, or as her Nanna had used to say, 'had been vaccinated with a gramophone needle'.

As she followed the directions to Kate's house, Grace hoped Lisa would be there. It bothered her that the lady was suffering and unhappy and Grace wanted desperately to be able to ease her pain. She knew too well the horror of a loveless and abusive marriage. She shuddered as she cast her mind back to the man she had left. I am well rid of you Jack Evans, she thought, lifting her hand to knock on the front door of what she hoped was Kate's house.

"So where is everyone?" Grace asked, as Kate ushered her into the living room.

"Oh it's just you and me. I didn't invite anyone else. Don't think my other mates will quite get it the same as you will."

Grace grew uneasy, scanning her eyes around the room for clues.

"Kate I don't understand. What do you mean? I thought your friends would be here too."

"Chill out, Grace. I didn't invite them because they aren't into all this paranormal stuff."

"Paranormal? Kate, I don't know anything about the paranormal," Grace said, as fear ran up her spine.

"Well it's not so much paranormal, just that I invited a medium round."

"A medium?! What on earth made you think I would be interested in seeing a medium?"

"Well I wanted to see one and I didn't want to do it on my own. I didn't think you would mind, given that you live with a ghost."

"OK Kate, this has gone far enough. I don't live with a ghost. It's you and Harry that keep telling me I live with a ghost. I don't believe in ghosts and I think this has all gotten way out of hand. You are both scaring me."

"Wooo, Grace, take a chill pill, hun. This is just a bit of fun, nothing serious. Don't see the medium if you don't want to. No one's gonna make you."

"I'm sorry, Kate. I overreacted. It's just that between you and Harry, ghosts seem to have become a living part of my life. I'm not comfortable with it. I don't believe in them."

"You know Grace, for a lady who doesn't believe in ghosts you sure seem pretty freaked out by them."

She was right and Grace knew it. If she really didn't believe in ghosts then none of this would be an issue. She would be sitting here enjoying a glass of wine and having a good laugh. The realization hit her like a bus and she stared open mouthed at her new friend.

"Kate, why did you arrange this?"

"I thought it would be fun and I wanted to see a medium."

"I don't believe you," Grace replied seriously.

"Yeah, alright, you rumbled me. Harry gave me her number this morning. He said you should see her. He knew you wouldn't go if he told you to so he asked me to set it up. I've got to be honest, it seems a bit strange. I mean you only met him on Friday. I know he is a nice guy and all that but this is just a bit weird, even for me. What's going on, Grace?"

Grace took a deep breath and wondered how much she should tell her new friend. So much of her new life depended on her relationship with Kate. She was her boss and one of only two friends she had. Could she really afford to risk all that by sharing the bizarre events that had become her life in the past few days?

"I don't know what is going on. I wish to God I did know, but I just don't. Kate, I am frightened," Grace said, as tears welled in her eyes.

Throwing her arms around her, Kate hugged her like a child. Tears rolled down her face as Grace sobbed and hugged her friend back.

"Shhh, hun, it's OK. I'm here."

"Kate, I just don't know what to do. It's all such a mess."

"What's a mess, Grace? Tell me, hun. I can't help you if I don't know what's wrong."

"Him... I mean, Robert Hamilton, the ghost. I don't know what he is. He is there in my head all the time. Wherever I go he is there. I sleep and he is in my dreams, I come to work and I see his face on the desk, I go to the pub and I see him behind the bar. Then Harry shows me this portrait of him and his wife. Kate, I'm in the portrait, I'm his wife."

Her boss drew back, her eyes staring fearfully at Grace.

"Oh my God, Grace! Do you know what this means?"

Grace shook her head slowly. As soon as the words had left her mouth she regretted them. She could see it in Kate's eyes. She had seen it before. The look a person had when they both pitied and feared someone. She had given too much away. Shared too much of herself. Of course her friend thought she was crazy. She thought she was crazy. Was this what schizophrenia felt like? Was that what was wrong with her? Jack had been right all along. She needed help, medication, something to control the delusions and hallucinations.

Grabbing for her handbag she made to leave.

"Kate... I'm sorry. I've got to go... I understand if you don't want me back at work tomorrow."

"Grace, hold on. What are you doing?"

"I've got to go," Grace said, hurriedly.

"Hold on, please. Don't go, my friend. We can fix this. I will help you."

Grace stood, clutching her handbag, staring at Kate.

"I thought you would want me to go."

"No. Why would I?"

"Because I am insane."

"That's a ridiculous notion. What makes you think that?"

"I'm seeing and talking to ghosts."

Kate smiled and gave a gentle laugh.

"When you put it that way... I guess you do sound a bit touched."

Grace's brow curved in a slight frown, her eyes filled with confusion and fear.

"So you do think I'm crazy?"

"No you daft beggar, of course I don't think you're crazy. I was joking. Look, Grace, this medium is due any minute. Go upstairs and sort your makeup out. I'll get us another glass of wine and then you can have a chat with the medium and we'll see if she can shed any light on all this."

Grace ran her finger nervously around the rim of the glass. Her friend sat beside her, perched on the edge of the settee, lazily balancing the bowl of the glass between her fingers.

"This is highly irregular. I don't usually have other people sit in on a reading," said the thin, wrinkled lady who had seated herself on the only single chair in the room.

"Anything you have to say to Grace you can say to both of us," said Kate, firmly.

The elderly lady raised her eyebrows at Grace.

"I want her to stay," Grace said to the medium.

"As you wish, but I can't be sure of an accurate session. It's going to throw the vibes right out, you both being here."

"We're willing to risk it," Kate said, irritated with the old lady's complaints.

The medium pursed her lips and a thin line of disapproval spread over her face. "Highly irregular this is, and don't you be coming to me later complaining the reading was wrong."

"We won't," both ladies chimed together.

"First grease the palm of an old lady's hand," she said, stretching out her hand. Grace reached for her handbag and ferreted clumsily for her purse, but Kate beat her to it, placing two twenty pound notes into the upturned hand.

"There you are old lady, now tell us what you can see," Kate said, moving back onto the settee beside her friend.

The medium stared at Grace, her eyes shifty and dark. Grace blinked and looked away. The old lady's searching eyes made her feel uncomfortable. A tension fell over the room as the medium continued to stare at Grace. 'Enough now,' she thought to herself as the minutes passed and the woman's eyes remained fixed on her face.

"Can you see anything," an impatient Kate asked.

The old woman ignored her.

Irritated, Grace stood up.

"This is nonsense, I've had enough."

"Sit down," the medium said, in a stern tone.

Grace did as she was told and sat down but wondered why she had. She felt like an animal in an experimental laboratory. She turned her head to her friend and raised her eyebrows.

"If you insist on moving all the time I won't be able to do my job. The sooner you sit still the sooner I will be done."

Grace obliged and turned to face the woman.

"You don't belong here," the old lady said abruptly. Grace drew a sharp breath. How could this woman know she had left Jack?

"You are married, but not to the one whose ring marks your finger."

Instinctively Grace looked toward her left hand, fearful that she still wore her wedding ring, but she had left it on Jack's bedside table. Her fingers were bare.

"What do you mean?" Kate asked.

The medium ignored her question again, shaking her head and muttering to herself.

"I told you this wouldn't work, not with two of you here. This isn't right, it's all wrong."

"Just tell us what you can see," Grace blurted in frustration.

"I can see you in your lover's arms, but ... beyond that... I'm sorry..."

"Sorry for what?" shouted Kate, "what is going to happen?"

"She will not exist, is no more... that is what ... she is going to die," the old lady said, clasping her trembling hands together.

Both girls stared in shocked silence at the old woman as she stuffed the twenty pound notes into her bra and rose unsteadily from the chair.

"Don't call me again until you are prepared to have individual readings," she said, making her way to the door. Without as much as a goodbye she opened the door and disappeared through it.

Grace lifted her glass to her mouth and drained the content.

"What the hell was that all about?" she asked, turning white-faced toward Kate.

"I am so sorry, Grace. I can't imagine what Harry was thinking getting you to see her. If I had known she was a nutcase I would never have gone along with it. Take no notice of her, Grace. It was rubbish, all of it. You said yourself you don't believe in all this."

Grace rubbed her forehead. She felt emotionally exhausted and engulfed by an ache that filled her whole body with a deep sense of foreboding.

"Kate I think it's time I went home. It's getting late and I'll never be up in the morning if I don't get to bed soon."

Her friend rested her hand gently on her shoulder. "Take the day off, Grace. We are on top of things; I will manage just fine tomorrow."

The moon glistened like a crystal in the night sky, illuminating the ancient city as she traced her steps back to her hotel. The hotel manager was sitting at the reception desk, still reading his crime thriller. Grace nodded and smiled politely. His eyes peeped over the top of the book; she didn't need to see his mouth to know it held a smile.

"Good evening, Mrs. Evans?"

She had hoped he wouldn't engage her in conversation but, now that he had, she found the sound of his voice reassuring.

"Yes thank you. How's your book?"

"Oh it's very good."

"Great things, books. I don't know what I would do without them," Grace said, thinking how utterly lost she would be without her books.

"That they are. The missus used to say they kept me out of trouble," he said, with a gentle laugh.

The sound of his laughter lifted her spirits and she felt a smile creep onto her lips.

"Good night, George. Enjoy the rest of your story," she said, heading for the stairs that would take her to her room.

"Night Mrs. Evans."

Back in her room she enjoyed a warm shower and a cup of coffee before sliding into bed. Too tired even to read, she kissed the photograph of her daughter and let her head fall heavily onto the pillow. The room was dark save for a tiny thread of moonlight which beamed through a gap in the curtains.

She lay staring at the light, replaying the words of the medium in her mind. What possessed the woman to say a thing like that she had no idea. If she had been trying to scare her, she had done a good job, but even as paranormal entertainment, Grace felt the old lady had gone too far.

As for Harry, she couldn't work out what he was trying to do. The man had seemed so kind, so eager to help her. It was all starting to look a lot like an old man getting his jollies by playing with other people's minds. Grace had been here before, experienced firsthand the fear and confusion mind games caused. Jack was a master of them. He had frequently twisted reality to play with her mind. Did she wear a sign with the word 'Mug' on her forehead? Was it just a fact of life that some people were born to provide entertainment for others? She didn't know, but as the hazy fog of sleep swept over her she decided that she would use her day off to find out once and for all who this Robert Hamilton was and what Harry and Kate were up to.

******

CHAPTER 5

She walked through a heavy dusk. Flakes of falling snow blew into her face. She lifted her hand to brush them away but there were too many. Her path ahead was clouded with a thick floating curtain of white. Gradually the dusk became evening and an unearthly orange glow fell over the city. Her body surged forward, driven by a mixture of fear and excitement.

She had to find him because her life depended on it. She searched the faces of the people around her, she checked down each tiny alley, every nook and cranny but he was nowhere to be found. The snow fell heavier and the pavements became covered until each step was labored.

Why hadn't he come to her? Every other night, he had come, but tonight when she needed him the most he had left her to search alone for him. As dusk became dawn she plunged through the bitterly cold wall of snow and fog. The air pierced her skin like a blade, her bones ached with weariness and her feet and hands numbed as darkness descended.

Her eyes sprang open and she stared at the ceiling, gasping for breath. Her heart pounded and her hands trembled. She was alive but she hadn't expected to be. There was an icy chill in the room that told her that either the radiator wasn't working or someone had turned it off.

Grace sat up slowly, pulling the duvet up under her chin to ward off the cold. She had slept late, later than she had in years. She slid out of bed and headed for the kettle. How much had she drunk at Kate's last night? Too much judging by the way she felt this morning. Her dream, the medium, they had all merged together into one muddled memory.

She poured her coffee and swallowed a painkiller with her first sip. Still trembling, she made her way back to bed. Never had she been so grateful for a chance to go back to bed. Her stomach churned and every movement brought her closer to being sick. Her head sank gratefully into the softness of the pillow and she closed her eyes tightly against the bright morning light.

She watched him as he removed his cufflinks and placed them neatly on the table beside the bed. He removed his shirt and dropped it on the chair beside him. His movements were labored and slow, his face drawn and tired. Her eyes travelled over him as he reached for a towel and rubbed it over his hair. Only then did she realize that he was wet. Suddenly he stopped and lifted his head toward her.

"Come here?" he whispered.

She slid across the bed toward him. The powerful muscles of his arms holding her tightly against him, she clung to him so hard that she struggled to breathe. Her heart pounded against him as great rivers of tears flowed from her eyes.

"Help me, please? I don't know what to do."

"Have faith my dearest Grace, for I will come for you. As sure as the dusk that will fall tonight, I will find you."

Feeling infinitely better for her sleep, Grace showered and set out in search of some much needed food. A bowl of pasta later and she felt ready to face the world again. Her plans for the afternoon included a trip to York Castle Museum. She didn't know why, only that it seemed a good idea. Life had become so complicated that reason and logic were long since forgotten.

The museum was mercifully quiet as Grace made her way slowly past each exhibit. She savored each one, trying to read as many of the information plaques as she could but the afternoon drew quickly to an end and the time fast approached when the museum would shut. She made her way quickly to the seventeenth century exhibits and displays. Most of the information was fairly generic but she scanned it all, eager not to miss anything.

She was drawn to a small display cabinet tucked in the corner of the museum. It held a few items, none of which looked terribly unique or particularly interesting except for a pair of lady's shoes that caught her eyes. They looked old but their design was modern. They might be four hundred years old but I wouldn't mind a pair of shoes like that, she thought to herself. Curious about their origin she searched the cabinet for the appropriate information tag.

'A pair of seventeenth century shoes worn by Grace Hamilton, wife of Robert Hamilton.'

She gasped and covered her mouth with her hand. Instinct told her to run. She felt exposed and afraid that someone would know who she was. Breathing deeply she told herself that she was being silly. No one was going to believe the ridiculous notion that she was Robert Hamilton's wife. The man had lived four hundred years ago. His wife was dead and buried alongside him. The thought made her stomach lurch, fear rippled up her spine and the memory of the headstone with the missing inscription burned in her eyes. She rubbed her forehead thoughtfully, wondering if there might be more information on Robert Hamilton in the museum. Her search was quickly rewarded. A pewter mug stood proudly in a display labeled *Pubs of York'*.

'A pewter mug, believed to have belonged to Robert Hamilton.'

She ran her fingers over the glass of the cabinet, tracing a slow line around the mug. She pictured his broad hand wrapped around the handle; his lips as the rim touched his mouth. She ached to touch him; to have him take her in his arms, as he had in her dream. But the ancient mug was a pitiful reminder that the man was long since dead and that her mental stability was very much in question.

She had read about people whose minds created their own reality. Again she considered the possibility that she might be schizophrenic. Were Harry and Kate even real? Did that information card really have her name on it? She guessed that it was perfectly possible that she had had a breakdown of some sort after arriving in York.

Perhaps this was her mind's way of coping and none of this was real. She had to admit that the idea of a fabricated reality made more sense than anything else she could think of. Grace shook her head in frustration. She wasn't sure she cared too much anymore. If she were indeed going insane then she wasn't about to die. Her dreams of Robert Hamilton were exquisite. She longed for the light they brought to her life, the happiness she felt when she was in them. The only thing that was destroying her life was her attempt to make sense of it all.

Grace completed her tour of the museum in considerably better spirits than she had started it. Relenting to her madness had proved liberating and she embraced every mention of Robert Hamilton, allowing her heart to leap with excitement with each new discovery about him.

She learnt that he was born in York and that he had two brothers and one sister and that at least one of his brother's descendents still lived in York. She wasn't surprised to discover that the descendent owned the same post house that Robert had. Of course, it was Harry. Her mind connected the dots and, as it did, her spirits lifted. Life had become a lot easier since she had ceased to question her sanity.

She didn't care if Harry or Kate were real; she had no idea whether her job was real or imagined or if she was even in York. Regardless, she decided it would be rude not to tell Kate that she wouldn't be going into work in the morning. She knew it was a liberty to take another day off so soon after starting. But what did it matter if the job didn't exist in the first place? She planned to spend tomorrow in the library where she intended to do further research on her Mr. Hamilton.

Back in her hotel room Grace reached across the desk and lifted the portrait off the wall.

"Right, Robert Hamilton. Time to have a good look at you."

She rested the portrait face up on the bed. It looked no different to the hundreds of other times she had stared at it over the past few days. A smile curled along her lips as she ran her finger gently over his wide square jaw. He was a handsome man, no wonder she had fallen so hopelessly in love with him. She saw the twinkle in his eyes as they smiled back at her and she sighed softly to herself. Soon she would sleep and then he would come to her again and she would cling to the dream as sure as if it were reality.

Lifting the portrait to the light she examined the frame. Even after so many years the gold leaf shone through. She turned it to the side and noticed some writing on the back of the canvas. Curious, she put the portrait back on the bed, face down. The writing was faded and difficult to make out so she reached for the bedside table lamp and brought it closer to the words.

"Dear Grace," it began. She recognized her own handwriting immediately. She had no memory of having taken this portrait off the wall and she certainly didn't recall ever writing on it. Confused and frightened she continued to read.

"Dear Grace," she began again. *"I know that you think you are insane, unstable and deranged and I also know that you won't believe this when I tell you that you're none of these things. You are having what you will know as a breakdown, but you will be alright in time with Robert's love and care.*

"Today you went to the York Castle Museum. You found a pair of shoes that Robert will make for you. Trust me; they are even more beautiful new. Harry is real and so is Kate. They are your friends, Grace. They won't hurt you.

'I want you to go the shops tomorrow and buy the largest backpack you can find. Try a good camping shop, you should find something suitable there. Then get yourself a good penknife, a lighter and a can of lighter gas, a box of candles, some ball point pens, a small sewing box, four hundred painkillers, (you will have to visit several chemists to get these), antiseptic cream, vitamin tablets, a couple of packs of knickers (they just don't have such things here and boy do you miss them when you don't have them), a block of chocolate, sugar cubes and granulated coffee. See if you can find two hot water bottles. Oh and buy yourself some of those nice fleecy jim jams as well.

"Grace I also need you to go and see Harry. Tell him to lift the floorboards in the small room next to the kitchen.

"And you need to tell Kate to open the bottom draw of the desk. It has a false bottom to it. Tell her to look underneath it.

"And Grace, don't go to see the doctor, you really don't need to.

"With much love from beyond time,
Grace Hamilton."

Grace stared at the writing in front of her, wondering how to cover up what she had done. Her heart pounded with the fear of discovery. What if George found this? She had defaced a four hundred year old portrait and didn't have the slightest memory of doing it.

Panicked, she lifted the frame and returned it to its place on the wall above the desk. She was going to have to register with a doctor; there was nothing else for it.

First thing tomorrow, she promised herself that she would find some help. As she slid in between the crisp white duvet and the cotton sheet she wondered where the doctors would send her. She couldn't possibly be allowed to roam the streets in this condition. She was a danger to herself and everyone around her.

For the first time since she had left Jack, Grace fumbled in her bag for the antidepressant tablets her doctor had prescribed. She popped the tiny tablet into her mouth knowing Robert would not come to her that night and she was right. He didn't.

A ray of brilliant sunlight streamed through the tiny gap where the curtains didn't quite meet. Grace rubbed her eyes as she fought to focus on her surroundings. She felt calmer and in more control than she had felt in days. The portrait still hung on the wall where she had left it last night, but the eyes of Robert Hamilton were veiled.

She remained curious about the character of the man who had filled her life for the past week and decided to stick to her plan and spend the day at the library. However she needed to find out if Harry and Kate existed and, if so, how much they had seen of her derangement.

Grace sighed, realizing the trip to the doctors would be necessary at some point but for today her old tablets had worked and she was back in control. She just had to remember that leaving Jack had not healed her. The tablets were an essential part of her life and without them she was very likely to end up institutionalized.

George was in his usual spot behind the reception desk. He smiled and lowered his book. It was a new one. He must have finished 'Bushfire'.

"Morning George, sleep well?"

"Good morning, Mrs. Evans. I did thank you, not enough of it though. How about you?"

"Actually George I did sleep well last night, thank you," she said. "I see you finished 'Bushfire'."

"I did, last night, after you came in. It was gone midnight before I got to bed."

Grace smiled, recalling how many books had kept her awake until the small hours of the morning.

"Tell me, George, how do you pronounce the title?" she asked, intrigued by the name on the cover of his new book.

"The Ca-ho-kian, I think. An American customer gave it to me a few weeks ago, said I should be sure to read it."

"Well enjoy your new book, George and I'll see you later."

She found the Olde Starre Inne off Stonegate, so that was real enough. What she didn't know yet was whether Harry existed or not. She appeared to have no way of distinguishing reality from fantasy.

Relief swam over her as she recognized Harry behind the bar, his cheerful face one large smile. That, she thought, was the first hurdle overcome.

Cautiously, Grace made her way toward the man suspiciously. His eyes shone as she approached the bar, and she let out a deep sigh, realizing that she had been holding her breath.

"Grace, I have been trying to get hold of you. Kate told me what happened on Monday night. I am so sorry, girl."

Immediately, Grace's heart sank as the experience of the medium came flooding back. Upset, she turned to leave but Harry rushed from behind the bar and grabbed hold of her arm.

"Hey, girl, don't go. Come and have a drink with an old man."

It would be rude to reject him and she couldn't see the harm in it. He only existed in her imagination anyway.

"OK, Harry, but I'm not bothered with anything strong. May I just have a coke please?"

"Course you can. Do you want diet or normal?"

"Normal, please, Harry. I could do with the sugar boost, besides all those sweeteners aren't good for you."

"Nor is sugar," he teased.

She smiled and took a seat at the bar. "I know, and I do drink the diet stuff but I know I shouldn't."

The pub was empty, just as it had been the first time she had been there, when she had seen Robert standing behind the bar, right where Harry was now. She smiled at the thought of his dark inviting eyes, the width of his shoulders and the long length of his taut toned thighs.

"What are you smiling at girl?"

"Oh, nothing, Harry, just a memory."

"Care to share it with me?"

She shook her head. "No, not today, but I do have a message for you."

His eyebrows lifted in question. "A message, hey. That sounds ominous."

"I don't know whether it is or not."

"Go on then, girl, what's it?"

"I'm to tell you to lift the floorboards in the small room next to the kitchen."

"Lift the floorboards? But why would I want to do that?"

"I have no idea and you don't have to do it. I'm just passing on a message."

"Funny thing messages."

"How so?"

Harry turned to Danny behind the bar.

"Do me a favor Danny, watch the bar for me. I've something that needs my attention. Grace, come with me, girl. I want to show you something."

Grace lifted her glass from the bar and slid off the high stool. She followed Harry through the pub and into the backrooms. He led her up the stairs and into the living quarters. He groaned as he bent and pulled the portrait of her and Robert from under the bed.

"Here, take a look at the portrait."

Grace took the frame from him, examining the picture. It was as she had remembered it; a painting of her and Robert done some four hundred years ago.

"I can't see anything I haven't already seen on this, Harry."

"Take a look at the back of the portrait," he repeated.

Grace knew what was coming. She had defaced another portrait. But what she couldn't figure out this time was how she had managed to do it to this one. Fearfully, she turned it over and read the inscription out loud.

"Dear Harry,

"Grace is going to come and see you on the 15th December. It will be snowing outside when she arrives (that was for Grace's benefit as she is still convinced that she is mad). She will give you a message. Listen to her and act on it. As much for your own benefit as hers.

"Oh and Harry, your uncle Robert says to tell you that he had no idea you were family. Between you and me he is very proud of the way you run the pub. But I worry about how much whisky you are drinking. Please make Grace a promise that you will stop drinking?

"Your friend from beyond time,
Grace Hamilton."

She wasn't shocked. Grace was passed being shocked by anything anymore. She did agree with one sentiment from the letter however, and that was that Harry drank way too much.

"Well, what do you think of that then?"

"I think that I have gone crazy, Harry. You are just a figment of my imagination and I am somehow going around defacing seventeenth century portraits."

"I can assure you, girl, that I am as real as this here pub. As for defacing portraits, well you got me there because this certainly does sound as though you wrote it. But look at it, Grace. It's faded so much it is almost impossible to make out the words. But they're your words and they're written with a modern hand and a modern pen. I would say, at a guess, a ballpoint pen."

She had to agree. The writing was faded and so were the words on the portrait in her room. She had neither the skill nor the knowledge to artificially age ink.

"What do you think it all means?" she asked, wide eyed and confused.

"Not being a genius or anything, I am going to make an educated guess: Grace, you are going to go back in time."

The idea wasn't foreign to her. She had repeated it to herself over the past week more times than she cared to remember. But that didn't make it any less ridiculous.

"Well that is all fine and dandy as an idea and it's not a bad fantasy. But please tell me how I am supposed to go back in time?"

Harry smiled and shrugged.

"I don't know Grace, but I do know that I was just told to listen to your message, so how's about we shut up the pub and go lift a few floorboards."

"You know, Harry, I have some shopping to do, the library to go to and I would also like to get to see Kate this evening. I'm gonna leave you to it, if you don't mind. Those boards have been down for four hundred years and I don't think it will take you just five minutes to shift them."

"Right you are, girl," he said, moving to hug her. "You take care of yourself, now. Do you hear me?"

Grace nodded and hugged him back. "I'll pop in after work tomorrow and see what you found. It's all very exciting."

"Danny lock up fella. I'm shutting up shop for the day. I'll give you a call when I need you back," Grace heard Harry shout as she left the front courtyard of the pub.

When Grace emerged onto Stonegate she was shocked to find that the gentle snowfall of earlier had turned into quite a blizzard. She shivered and pulled the collar of her coat up around her neck. It was ten days before Christmas and the city heaved with the traditional bustle of the season. She looked up at the string of lights that adorned the street. They looked so beautiful when they came on.

Christmas always took her mind back to her childhood. She supposed it must do the same for everyone. There was nothing in this world as exciting as the fantasy of Father Christmas. She sighed at the memory of how simple life had seemed back then. Children don't question, they just blindly accepted, she thought, watching a young mother hurrying down Stonegate with her little boy's hand tightly clutched in hers.

The snow fell heavier as she made her way through the city, purchasing the items listed on the back of the portrait. She wondered dimly what they were for; but her mind was so far past the point of reason that she lost the thought almost as fast as she had it.

The oversized backpack grew heavier until its weight on her back became a burden. She slung both straps over her shoulders and proceeded through the city.

Night was falling fast and the pavements had become almost impassable with snow. Her shoes were totally unsuitable for the conditions and her feet burned with the cold. She headed away from the city and toward Kate's house.

Everything looked so different with a thick covering of snow on the ground. The house came into view. Grace made her way toward the door and knocked. A few moments later, Kate answered.

"Grace! Are you OK?"

"I'm fine. Do you mind if I come in?"

"No, of course I don't mind. Sorry, come in Grace. You look soaked to the skin."

Kate took Grace's hand and pulled her through the door into the warmth of the hallway.

"What on earth are you doing? No one should be out in this. Why didn't you get a taxi? Do you want a glass of wine?"

Grace nodded, wrapping her arms around herself trying to warm up. She moved to stand in front of the radiator, lifting her hands over the gentle heat that radiated from it. Her fingers burnt and she knew there was a reason she shouldn't keep her hands in the heat but her mind had forgotten that reason and the only coherent thought she could manage was that she needed to get warm.

"Here you go, hun. Get this down you, it's mulled wine. It'll warm you up nicely," she said, handing Grace a large warm glass of red wine. "I haven't boiled it, just heated it a bit."

"Thanks, Kate. This is lovely," she said, taking a sip of the warm liquid and enjoying the heat it brought to her as it slid down the back of her throat.

"You know, Grace, don't take this the wrong way hun, but you look dreadful. Are you still feeling rattled by that silly old bat from Monday night?"

Grace shook her head and took another sip of the warm wine.

"No, I'm fine, honestly. Nothing a good night's sleep won't fix."

"Are you still having trouble sleeping in that room?"

"No. Honest Kate, I'm absolutely fine. As I said, just need a good night's sleep and I'll be good as new."

Grace emptied the last of the liquid from the glass.

"Want some more?"

"That would be nice, thanks."

"Fancy watching a film?" Kate asked, returning with two filled glasses.

"I can't. It's getting late and the weather is dreadful. I only came for a quick chat."

"No worries, Grace. Anything in particular you wanted to chat about?"

"Well actually there was. It's about your desk; you know the one that Robert made his wife."

"You mean the one that he made for you?"

"Don't mess around, Kate. That's just daft and we both know it."

"How so? You know Harry believes you are going to go back in time."

"Think about what you are saying. It's not possible. No one has ever done it."

"No one that you know about. People go missing all the time."

"Yes, they do. I did it myself, but I've not travelled in time. I just left my husband and moved to York."

"I wondered what happened. Thought it might be something like that but I didn't like to ask. Figured you would tell me when you were ready."

"I hadn't intended to tell anyone. I hope you will keep it to yourself, Kate. Jack is a dangerous man and I can't risk him finding me."

"Your secret is safe with me, hun. I promise, I won't tell a living soul."

"Thank you."

"No worries. But it won't matter one day because you won't be here anymore."

"There is the chance the medium was right," Grace said, feeling the sick knot in her stomach tighten.

"I don't mean that you're going to die, you muppet. You'll be four hundred years in the past. He's hardly likely to find you there."

"Enough, Kate. It won't happen."

"If you say so. Here, give me your glass and I'll get us both another."

Grace stared as the lights on the Christmas tree flashed in her eyes. They blurred and the colors blended like a halo around the tree. She could see the hazy outline of his face forming in the glow. His eyes found her and a gentle smile spread across his face. She lifted her hand and stretched her fingers toward him.

"I love you," he whispered as the hazy outline of his features started to fade.

"Here you go, Grace," Kate said, handing her friend the filled glass.

Grace took the glass from her but continued to stare, unblinking at the tree.

"Mesmerizing, aren't they?" Kate said, sitting cross-legged on the floor.

Grace blinked and the image faded. She was suddenly aware of the sound of the wind howling against the window.

"I'd better not be too much longer, it sounds nasty out there."

"You want me to call you a taxi?"

"No, it's not far. I'll be fine."

"You sure?"

Grace nodded and took a few sips from the glass.

"Can I use your bathroom before I leave?"

"Course, it's up there."

Grace picked up her bag and made her way toward the stairs. She shuddered as a gust of wind lashed against the landing window. 'I certainly hope it's stopped snowing out there,' she thought to herself as she made her way into the bathroom.

She looked at herself in the mirror above the sink. Her cheeks were sunken and her skin pale and grey. She turned the tap on and splashed cold water onto her face. It left the sting of a slap on her cheeks but she felt better for it. Opening her bag she found the antidepressant tablets. She popped one out of its blister and dropped the tablet into her mouth.

"Feeling a bit better?" Kate asked as Grace returned to the room.

"A bit, thanks," she said, reaching for the backpack. "Kate, before I go, I have a message for you."

"OK, who from?"

"Well I can't really tell you that."

"Right," replied her friend a little skeptically, "Can I just ask if Harry is behind this?"

"This has nothing to do with Harry, although I did have a message for him as well."

"Cool. So what's the message then?"

"It's... just that, you know the drawer in your desk?"

"Which one?"

"One of the lower drawers, it has a false bottom to it."

"Wow, who would figure? I've had that desk for years and I had no idea. How on earth did you find out?"

"Don't ask. It's a long story. I've got to go now. It's late and the weather's getting worse. Just lift the false bottom of the drawer."

"OK, hun, I'll lift it, promise. Now you look after yourself out there. Give me a ring when you get back to the hotel. Just to let me know you got there safely."

"Yeah, sure, will do," she said, doing up the buttons on her coat and slinging the backpack over her shoulder. "Kate, would you mind if I take tomorrow off? I think I should see a doctor."

"That's fine, hun. Things have slowed down a bit the last few days because of Christmas."

The wind howled around them as they hugged goodbye on the doorstep.

"You sure I can't call you taxi?"

"I'll be fine. Go on, get back inside, Kate, you'll catch your death out here."

Kate laughed, "And you won't? Come on, Grace, let me get you a taxi."

"Really, I'm fine," she said, giving her friend a final quick wave before turning toward the street.

Quickly disorientated by the dense fog and carpet of snow that blanketed the city, she found herself on a street that she didn't recognize. Tired and struggling through the deep snow, she wished she had worn her boots instead of her trainers.

Icy wind pounded her with snow, the air pierced her skin like a blade and the cold snow burnt her feet through her trainers as she plunged through the bitter blizzard. She blinked, trying to clear her streaming eyes and stumbled with the weight of the backpack. The snow-covered street was deserted but she cried for help nonetheless. The weak pitiful wail was swallowed by the howling wind as she stumbled again and fell to the ground.

Tiredness crept into every muscle and bone of her body. She could hear the thudding of her pulse in her ears, felt the bitter cold of the snow beneath her hands and knees as she crawled along the ground. Terror gripped her as she sank exhausted into a snow drift. In desperation she tried to pull herself up, but the ache and weariness in her limbs prevented her from rising. Stuck on her hands and knees with the weight of the bag on back she noticed her crystal necklace swinging from her neck and illogically started concentrating on the pendulum swing of the crystal, forgetting all about trying to stand. There was a flash of lightening followed immediately by a clap of thunder that seemed to knock her to the ground, forcing all the air from her lungs.

The falling snow started to spin, forming an ever-tightening vortex of darkness around her, made all the worse by the recent blinding flash of lightening. She could hear the murmur of a voice somewhere in the distance as she desperately fought to keep herself from sleep. Her arm reached out in the direction of the voice and her fingers stretched to touch its source.

In those final moments of life she felt his arm around her shoulders, his face so close that his breath warmed her cheeks. She heard the gentle rumble of his voice tremble in her ears as she clawed at the tiny hole of light, desperate to break through the darkness.

As life drifted from her body and all conscious thought became dreams, her mind clung to the hazy image of Robert Hamilton.

He lifted her lifeless body and carried her through the blizzard toward the city lights. Deterred by the late hour, driving wind and heavy snowfall most residents had abandoned the streets for the comfort of a warm fire and the shelter of their homes.

Robert was grateful for the deserted streets and late hour as he approached the door of his house. He would have had a hard time explaining the limp body in his arms to anyone who might have enquired. Not to mention the strange looking sack he had found on her back.

Gently he placed her on the mattress of his bed. He lifted his hand and brushed his knuckles slowly over her cheek. He watched the shallow rise and fall of her chest and knew, as sure as the sun that had just set, that she clung to life by a thread.

Undeterred by propriety he removed her sodden clothes and covered her gently with the padded quilt from his bed. He placed a warmed brick wrapped in a cotton cloth at her feet and stoked the fire in the room, before removing his own sodden clothes and toweling his hair dry. Reaching for a clean shirt and trousers he hurriedly dressed so that he could examine the sack he had found her with.

He couldn't find an opening to the sack and assumed it had been stitched all round. He was puzzled by the strange leather and cloth that had been used to make it. His eyes wandered over her discarded clothes and her ruined shoes. He raised her hand gently and examined the bracelet on her left wrist. It looked to Robert like a timepiece, but he had never seen one so delicate and small. He rested her hand on his upturned palm and brushed his lips across her fingers. He wrapped his hand around hers and clutched it tightly to his chest.

She gasped as her body sprang back to life. Her eyelids flickered as she fought to open them. She could feel him beside her, clutching her hand to his chest. She could hear the crackle of a fire and the howling of the wind as it lashed against the window. She was in a familiar yet strange place. Her heart raced with anticipation as her eyes opened to the recognition of Robert Hamilton.

"Who are you and why have you haunted me so?" he whispered.

"I've been haunting you? You've got to be bloody joking," Grace said, sitting bolt upright in the bed. Realizing too late that she had nothing on, Grace grabbed for the blanket and pulled it up underneath her chin. "Where the hell are my clothes?"

He raised his brows, casting his eyes lazily toward the wrought iron bedstead where Grace's clothes hung neatly.

"They were wet," he replied simply.

"So you just decided to take them off?"

"You were catching your death."

She stared at him, her mind replaying what he had just said.

"Wet? You just said my clothes were wet?"

He nodded solemnly, a slight frown creasing his brow.

"I found you, face down in the snow."

Color drained from her face, her eyes frantically scanned the dimly lit room around her.

"Am I dead?"

"No."

A surge of panic ripped through her.

"Then I'm dreaming... which means I'm probably still lying face down in the snow," she said, panic causing her voice to quiver. "I've got to wake up. Help me Robert! Help me wake up!"

"You aren't dreaming."

"I am! You've got to help me or I'm going to die."

"You are not going to die."

"I am! No one will find me. The snow is too heavy."

Her heart pounded and her head throbbed as she tried desperately to work out how to wake herself.

He rose from the chair and stood beside the bed taking her shoulders in his large hands and holding her firmly.

"You are not going to die and you are not dreaming. Do you hear me?"

She could feel his warm breath on her face and a shiver passed through her at the touch of his hands on her bare shoulders.

"If I'm not dreaming and I'm not dead, what am I?"

Gently he let go of her and perched himself on the edge of the bed.

"That's what I would like to know," he whispered.

"Where am I?" she asked softly.

"In my bed."

"That's not terribly helpful," she said, growing irritated with his curt replies.

"Why don't you start by telling me what you were doing out in that snowstorm?" he asked.

"Why don't you start by telling me what you are doing here when you're supposed to be dead?" she snapped.

"And what makes you think I should be dead?"

"You died four hundred years ago."

"Did I?" he said, raising his brows in mock surprise.

"Yes, you did."

"Well then, you are probably right. I should be dead."

"But you're not?"

"Very observant of you, Grace."

"How do you know my name?"

"I don't know. But I could ask the same of you."

"I know your damn name because of that portrait," she said, pointing to the picture above the mantle.

He turned slowly to look at the portrait.

"You have seen this portrait before?"

"Yes, I have seen your portrait and to tell you the truth I am growing quite sick of it. It has brought me nothing but grief since I first laid eyes on it."

"I am very interested to know where you have seen this portrait, considering it has never left this room."

"It's true," she whispered with horror as her mind rationalized fantasy into probable reality.

"What is true?"

"All this," she said, pointing around the room. "I don't belong here. I'm not where I should be."

"Where should you be, Grace?"

"At home... I don't know," she replied, pathetically, realizing mid-sentence that she had no idea where home was anymore.

He shifted off the bed and moved toward a trunk in the corner of the room. Opening it, he removed a cream cotton shirt.

"Here, put this on," he said, handing her the shirt and turning his back to her.

Grateful for the offer, Grace wasted no time slipping the shirt over her head. Getting out of bed she moved to stand in front of the fire.

Robert came to stand beside her.

"Here, drink this," he said, holding a pewter mug out for her.

"What is it?" Grace asked, as she recognized the mug from York Castle Museum.

"Whisky."

"Oh, not again. It must be hereditary," she sighed, waving the mug cautiously under her nose.

"You don't like whisky?"

"No, but I'll drink it."

He laughed softly. "I have no doubt you will."

Grace lifted her head and raised her eyes to look at the portrait.

"I'm not a witch," she said, suddenly.

"I didn't say you were."

"But you must be thinking it."

"I don't believe in witches."

"You don't?"

"No. I don't."

"I thought everyone believed in witches in the seventeenth century."

"It seems you believed wrong," he said, turning to face her, "You're not from this time are you?"

"No."

"Did you intend to come here?"

"No... No, I didn't intend to come here."

"Do you know how you got here?"

Slowly she turned from the fire to face the man standing beside her.

"No, but I did know I was coming."

"I don't suppose you would care to share what you know with me," he asked.

"You won't believe it."

"Try me, Grace," he said, his voice so low she could hardly hear him.

She lifted the mug to her mouth and swallowed the content. He slapped her on the back as she gasped and choked on the fumes from the liquid.

"Sorry," she said, still trying to catch her breath.

The corner of his lips quirked in a gentle smile that reached his eyes.

"Another?"

She shook her head fervently.

"I didn't think so," he said, pouring himself another.

Grace sat on the rug in front of the fire, playing nervously with the oversized sleeves of the cotton shirt.

Robert sank to the floor beside her, and propped himself up on his elbow, his mug resting on his bent knee. He stared at her for a while, his eyes searching intently.

"What do you know, Grace?"

She took a deep breath, filling her lungs with much needed air.

"I was born and grew up in Derbyshire about four hundred years from now. I married a man called Jack Evans and we have a daughter. My husband is a cruel and evil man, or he will be... I left him a little over a week ago and moved to York," she paused, taking her eyes off the flames of the fire and turned to face Robert.

"You won't understand any of this. In your time a man can do as he wishes with a woman. Things are different in my time. Women have a voice."

He raised his brows and lifted the mug of whisky to his mouth.

"I have great respect for the women in my family," he said, pausing as the liquid slid down his throat. "I don't believe they are capable of fighting wars or chopping wood. But then there are many roles they perform that I cannot. I would no more ignore my mother's voice than I would my father's. Don't presume to judge me, Grace."

"I'm sorry. I just assumed you wouldn't understand."

"If I don't understand you, I will say so."

"OK," she said, nodding slowly.

"So you fled to York a week ago?" he said, prompting her to continue.

"Yes, I fled to York and when I got there I was lonely and frightened. It was getting dark when I got off the train..."

"Train?" he interrupted her.

"It's a way of traveling... like a large carriage," she said.

"So you used this train to get you to York?"

She nodded. "I was at the bottom of the steps of the Minster when I spotted the Cavalier."

"You have Cavaliers still?"

Grace laughed and her mood immediately lightened.

"The Cavalier is a hotel, Robert. It's this place four hundred years in the future."

"So you took a room in my house?"

"I did and what's more, I stayed in this very room."

"My room?"

"Yes, Robert, your room, and your portrait is still there. But the fireplace has been boarded up."

"They boarded up the fireplace?"

"There is no need for them."

"Do they not have cold winters anymore?"

"Oh yes, the winters are just as cold but they have different ways to heat rooms. They pump hot water into metal panels. The panels get hot and that heat works just as well as a fire does today, even better in most cases."

"I think I will keep my fire," he said, skeptically.

She watched his eyes as they sparkled in the gentle light of the flames. A frown of confusion veiled them and the hint of something else, something she couldn't identify, hid in their depths.

"So you have been sleeping in my room?"

"Well not exactly sleeping, thanks to that portrait... and you," she said, rising from the floor and looking up at the portrait.

"Me? How, Grace? How have I disturbed your sleep?" he said, standing and moving closer to her. They stared at each other, his eyes glistening in the firelight.

Holding her gaze, he placed his mug firmly on the mantle.

"Tell me, Grace? How can a man you have never met disturb your sleep?"

His face was so close that she could smell the whisky on his breath; his lips hovered inches from hers. His hand cupped her cheek and then his long, strong finger trailed the line of her jaw coming to rest beneath her chin. His finger tilted her face and she swayed slightly. He put his hands around her waist and pulled her gently against him. She could feel the taut muscles of his chest against her, the racing of his heart, the warmth of his body and the strength of his arms around her.

"I... don't know."

"You don't know, or you don't understand?"

"I don't understand," she whispered breathlessly.

"Then perhaps we can come to understand?"

"Yes... perhaps, we can."

"But first Grace, I am going to kiss you," he said, suddenly pulling her hard against him. She gasped, tasting the smoky tang of his lips as they crushed down over hers, searching, desperate and yearning.

Then he released her gently, as if nothing had happened.

"Now," he said, "we may find understanding."

Her head felt light and dizzy as she sank back to the comfort of the rug on the floor. If history was right then she was going to marry this man. A man she barely knew but who, with just one kiss had filled the empty space that had been her shattered heart.

He crouched in front of the fire, dropping more wood into the flames. It cracked and popped as he dug the poker into the glowing embers. She noticed the hard contours of his body as he idly lifted the logs, the wide expanse of his shoulders, his broad back that tapered to a thin waist.

She had no doubt that this man had been a fighter and she shuddered at the thought of what that meant. How many men had he killed? She cast her eyes away from him and stared at the rug. Panic tightened in her stomach as the realization of where she was, and with whom, began to dawn.

"Why did you kiss me?"

He rose from the fire and lifted his mug off the mantle.

"Did you not like it?"

"I didn't say that."

"If you didn't dislike it then why question it?"

"Because I want to know what made you kiss me."

"You, Grace, you are what made me kiss you."

"Why won't you answer my question?"

"I just did."

"No, you didn't. You avoided my question."

He sank to the floor beside her on the rug, stretching his long legs out toward the fire and leaning back on his hands.

"Alright, Grace. I will answer your question. I kissed you because I wanted to make sure you were real."

"Oh, so you do think I'm a witch?"

"No. I have told you I don't believe in witches."

"So if you don't think I'm a witch what could possibly make you question whether I'm real or not?"

"Because you have haunted me, Grace. Day in and day out you are there. I close my eyes to sleep and you fill my dreams and now you are here and I will be dammed if I know what to do with you."

"Well if I'm so much trouble I'll just get my things and go," she said, making to rise from the rug.

He grabbed her arm and pulled her down.

"Firstly, I didn't say you were trouble and secondly you wouldn't survive long enough to get to the steps of the Minster. You have not the faintest idea where you are and despite what you think, you know nothing of the time you are in. You're not going anywhere."

She tried to pull away from him but he still had her arm in the firm grasp of his hand.

"I said you're not going anywhere. Now just sit down,"

"I did a history degree. I know more than you think I do about this time," she said, regretting them as soon as the words had left her mouth.

The sides of his mouth curled in a smile as he let go of her arm.

"Just sit down, Grace, please?"

Tears filled her eyes as she realized he was right. She was trapped in a time she didn't understand, with a man she didn't know and she had less idea than he did what she should do.

"Tell me what to do, Robert," she said, as tears broke free and ran freely down her cheek.

He moved toward her and brushed the tears from her face.

"I won't let anyone hurt you. You are safe here, Grace."

"But you don't want me here, how can I accept your help?"

"I never said I didn't want you here."

"You haven't exactly said you do either."

"Alright, then I shall say it. I want you here, Grace."

"Out of obligation and duty?"

"Why should I feel obliged or duty bound?"

"I don't know; because you found me, because you are an honest man and because you know I have nowhere else to go."

"Grace," he said, raising his finger to her lips, "stop. I want you here because I have longed to have you here. For nights I dreamt of you, held you in my arms and loved you."

Their eyes locked and she knew he told the truth, for she had dreamt the same.

"How did you know where to find me?"

"I heard your cry for help and when I looked I found you face down and covered with falling snow. Grace I am in love with you," he said, his voice thick and hoarse with desire.

She felt her breath catch in her throat, her pulse quickened and a wave of heat rose within her.

"And I with you, Robert."

"May I kiss you again?"

"Yes... yes, I would like that very much," she whispered breathlessly.

******

CHAPTER 6

Grace stirred as a gust of wind lashed the window. She nestled into his embrace, resting her head in the curve of his shoulder. A shiver rose up her body and his arm tightened protectively around her, cupping her small hand in his palm. He was instantly awake.

"Are you cold?"

"A little," she said, lifting her left hand to check her watch.

"It's nearly six o'clock."

"What of it?"

"Nothing, it's just that I'm used to getting up now."

"Then we shall rise," he said, removing his hand from hers and sliding out of bed.

She shivered as his movement produced a cold draft of air in the bed.

"Stay there."

"What are you doing?"

"Putting some logs on the fire."

"I could have done that."

"I've no doubt you could."

Sliding out the bed she lifted the top blanket and wrapped it around herself. Still shivering, she made her way to where Robert crouched in front of the fire.

"Aren't you cold?" she asked.

"No."

"But you've only got a pair of trousers... err, sorry, breeches on."

He turned his head from the fire and smiled up at her.

"What am I going to do with you?"

Offended, she shot him an accusing look.

"What do you mean?"

"What I mean, Grace, is that it's going to be the devil's own work keeping you out of trouble."

"What, just because I slipped up and called your breeches trousers?"

"Yes."

Flames hissed and danced around each other as another log was dropped into the fire, casting flickering shadows on the whitewashed walls of the room. Grace moved closer, holding her hands out to the flames. Robert sprung to her side, gently moving her away from the fire.

"What's wrong now?"

"If you stand that close to a fire with a blanket trailing on the hearth, it will catch fire."

She lowered her head to her feet and realized he was right. The edges of the woolen blanket hung wide and loose, trailing dangerously close to the flames.

"I'm sorry," she said, softly.

"You have done nothing wrong."

"I nearly set fire to your house."

A loud rumbling sound bellowed from his throat as he threw his head back and laughed.

"What?" she said, startled by his laughter. When he didn't answer she tried again. "What's so funny?"

He breathed deeply, choking on a final laugh before reaching out and drawing her into his arms.

"I do not care one tiny ounce for this building."

"But... you just said..."

"That I didn't want you to catch fire," he said, interrupting her mid-sentence.

"Oh," she replied, feeling rather silly, "I just assumed you meant the house."

"I know," he said, brushing his lips lightly over the top of her head. "Would you like something to eat?"

"Not really, but I would love a cup of coffee," she said, reaching for her backpack.

He watched her intently as she unzipped it and emptied the contents onto the bed. Triumphantly she held up the coffee, creamer and sugar.

"Robert Hamilton, you are about to taste heaven."

The side of his mouth quirked in a gentle smile.

"I already have. But I would be more than happy to taste it again."

Grace reached for a pillow and threw it at him. He caught it and threw it back at her.

"I meant this, you muppet," she said, laughing and holding up the jar of coffee. "Do you have any boiled water?"

"No, but I can arrange some."

"Not from the river."

His eyebrows raised in question.

"Is there any particular reason why the water can't be from the river?"

"There is."

"Well, do you care to share the reason with me?"

"Only if you promise not to laugh at me."

"Alright, I promise."

"The water in the river is vile."

"You haven't seen the rivers."

"No, I don't need to. The water in those rivers is dangerous and capable of killing us both, boiled or not. There is a well at the back of your posting house. Use that water."

He frowned down at her, confusion veiling his eyes.

"How do you know about my posting house and the well?"

"I told you, I did a history degree."

"And this degree qualified you in the ownership of buildings and location of city wells, did it?"

"No, I made it my business to find out."

"So you deem the water in my well safe to drink?"

"If it's boiled, yes."

Nodding, he pulled a cotton shirt over his head and moved toward the bedroom door.

"As it happens, there is a pail of well water downstairs. Coming?" he said, opening the door.

Grace followed him down the familiar stairs and into what would be the reception area of the hotel. She pulled the blanket tighter as the air pierced its weave. Through the thick window panes she could see a curtain of snow and fog. The wind still howled through the street and deep drifts had appeared against the buildings.

"It's so cold in here, Robert."

"It won't be once I get this going," he said, as he moved in front of the empty fireplace.

"Robert what am I going to do for clothes?" she said, clutching the woolen blanket under her chin.

Striking the flint over the straw, the kindling burst into flames and a gentle warming glow filled the room.

"I will get you some."

"But it takes months to make a single gown and I don't have any money to pay for one. I can't leave the house in jeans and a sweatshirt, so even if I did have the money to pay for one, I could hardly go in search of a seamstress."

"I have a sister. She can spare a gown until a new one can be made for you."

"I can't just ask your sister to lend me a dress."

"No, you can't. So I will ask her."

"You don't think she will take offence?"

"No, I don't, or I wouldn't ask her."

"I have nothing to give her in return."

"She won't want anything," he said, lifting a long black coat off the back of a wooden chair.

"What are you doing?"

"I'm going to get you a gown. The water is through there," he replied, pointing to a door.

As Robert opened the front door a gust of wind and snow howled into the room.

"Don't open this again until I return. Not for anyone, Grace."

She took his meaning well enough.

Without further comment he was gone. She cast her eyes around the room, so familiar yet so foreign. She pictured the elderly hotel owner, George, in the corner of the room, sitting behind the reception desk, his face nearly always hidden by the cover of a book. She thought of Harry and wished she could tell him he had been right. In truth, she still wasn't convinced. It was still entirely possible that her mind had created this entire scenario, or that she was in a dream or even dead. Time-traveling four hundred years into the past seemed the least plausible explanation. Her head hurt from trying to understand it all and just at that moment she didn't much care what had brought her to this place. She was happy, and despite all the uncertainty, Grace felt safe and with this thought she set about making her first cup of coffee in her new life.

An icy blast of air signaled Robert's return. White with snow, his hair limply framed the square line of his jaw. Carefully he draped the gown over the back of a chair and proceeded to remove his dripping coat.

"By God it's a foul wind that blows today. The streets are knee deep with lying snow. Much more of this and the city will be cut off for sure."

"Here, drink this," she said, handing him a mug of steaming hot coffee.

He cupped his hands around the mug, sniffing thoughtfully at its content.

"Smells good. Is this the coffee you were so eager to make?"

"It is," she said, with pride. "Go on, Robert, try it. Only don't go getting addicted to it, because I can't exactly pop back and fetch another jar when this is one is finished."

He laughed, bringing the mug up to his lips and taking a generous swig of the liquid. A contented sigh followed as he placed the mug on a table and opened a cabinet. Moments later he extracted a bottle from the cabinet and using his teeth, pulled a cork from the bottle. A liberal measure of its content was poured into the mug before he once more took a hearty swig of the coffee.

"Now that is a good drink," he said, smiling broadly at Grace as she stood staring open mouthed at him.

"How did you know to add whisky to the coffee?"

"What do you mean?"

"Well it's just something that people do in my time and I didn't expect you to know to do it."

"The people in your time have good taste."

"Perhaps, but how did you know to add whisky to your coffee?"

"You make too much of it, Grace. It tastes good, no?"

"Well I don't like it in coffee but then I don't like whisky, but thousands of other people do, so I guess it must."

"Then the reason for doing it isn't important. Sarah said you could have this gown and I've got a cobbler coming around later to make a start on some boots for you."

"I hadn't thought about shoes, but I guess I can't exactly go around in trainers."

"Trainers?"

"That's the name of the shoes I was wearing. They are probably ruined from the snow anyway."

"Yes, I'm afraid your shoes didn't look like they were going to be much use to you anymore. Odd leather they use in your time."

"It's not leather. They call it plastic. It's kinda complicated but basically plastic is a material that is made from oil and oil is extracted from the ground. Odd concept, huh?"

"Not so odd a concept but I do think the shoes are ugly."

Grace laughed. "You know the castle?"

He nodded, "What of it?"

"In my time, it's a museum... a place where people can go and see things from the past. Anyway, there are a couple of displays there dedicated to you.

"To me?" he said, surprised.

Grace nodded, "Yes, to you, Robert. Yesterday I saw a pair of shoes there that you have made for your wife."

Robert frowned in confusion. "I don't have a wife."

"Not yet you don't."

"What does that mean?"

"I can't tell you."

"That's nonsense."

"No, it's not. I shouldn't have started this conversation. I'm sorry. Please don't press me on it. I can't tell you."

"Will you tell me one day?"

"Perhaps."

"Robert what did you tell your sister about me?" she said, changing the subject.

"I told her that you are my wife."

"Your wife? But won't she wonder why you didn't tell her you married? Or why I have nothing to wear?"

"Grace, sit down," he said, pausing to allow her to do as he had asked. "Sarah is deliriously happy for me and hasn't questioned a thing I have told her. As far as she and the rest of this city are concerned, you are from Derbyshire and I married you two weeks ago at St Mary's church in Chesterfield."

"Did you just say St Mary's church in Chesterfield?"

"I did?"

"Do you know Chesterfield then?"

"Well I know it in this time. I'm afraid I can't offer much of an opinion on what it is like in your time. Grace, you need to know what I have told Sarah," he said, bringing her back to their original conversation. "We married in Chesterfield, two weeks ago. I sent a private coach to transport you to York and last night, just outside the city, your coach overturned in the snow and you were robbed by highway men."

"You're not just a very handsome man are you?"

"No?"

"No, you're smart as well," she said, dropping the blanket from her shoulders and moving to stand in front of him.

His eyes travelled from her face down the length of her body, lingering where the cotton shirt swelled over the rise of her breasts. One dark brow lifted.

"And you are a beautiful woman who is going to teach me many things," he whispered, in a deep and husky rumble. A faint smile touched his lips. "But first you need to take that shirt off. The cobbler will be here soon. Here," he said, lifting the gown from the back of the chair, "go and put this on... oh and, Grace, remove that bracelet from your wrist."

******

CHAPTER 7

He shut the door and stood with his back against it. Grace lifted her head toward him and lazily stretched her legs out in front of the fire.

"It went well with the cobbler," he said, staring intently across at her.

She weighed his words, trying to decide if he was joking or being serious.

"I suppose it did. If you don't count the strange looks the man kept giving me. I do believe your cobbler thinks I am a little odd."

"You are a little odd," he said, laughing.

She scowled up at him. "That's not very nice."

"Grace just under twenty four hours ago you travelled nearly four hundred years into the past. That's a little odd even by my reckoning."

Her face lost its scowl and she too laughed. He moved to sit beside her on the floor.

"Would you care to share?"

"Share?"

"Your thoughts."

"Oh, sorry. I was thinking about my daughter."

"You have a child?"

Grace nodded and reached for her purse. "Jenny," she said, showing the photograph to Robert.

"That's an impressive portrait," he said.

"It's not really a portrait, it's called a photograph."

"Whatever it's called, it's very good. You have a beautiful daughter."

"Thank you."

"I need to open the posting house tomorrow. Would you like to come with me?"

Grace slid the photograph back into her purse.

"Yes, Robert, I would like that very much," she said, wiping a single tear from her cheek.

For a moment, Grace was paralyzed with fear. Despite the deep lying snow, the city bustled around them.

"What if they suspect?" she whispered.

"No one is going to know, Grace. Just relax," he said, reaching for her hand and tucking it safely in his.

With her free hand she tried to hoist her skirts up, out of the snow, but it was too deep and the hem became soaked. It clung to her legs, wet and heavy around her calves. The icy wind whipped around her ears and Grace started to shiver violently with the cold. Robert wrapped his arm around her for warmth, hurrying her along the street until finally they were on Stonegate.

"Nearly there."

"I know," she replied, through chattering teeth.

He slid the key into the lock, turned it and swung the door open, pushing her through it.

"I'll get the fire going."

The post house was in complete darkness but Robert moved swiftly toward the fireplace and set to work immediately on a fire.

"There are some blankets upstairs and a lamp on the bar."

Her eyes adjusted quickly to the darkness and she spotted the lamp easily enough. Reaching into her pocket she extracted a lighter and lit the wick. Robert vaulted to his feet and spun round to face her.

"What are you doing?"

"I'm just lighting the lamp. Why? What's wrong?"

"Grace you can't do that. You must never do that again. Do you hear me?"

She nodded fervently but didn't understand.

"What have I done, Robert? I don't understand."

"Whatever you just used to light that wick, doesn't belong here, Grace. It looks like magic."

Her eyes widened as realization dawned.

"I didn't think, I'm... sorry."

He nodded and held out his hand.

"I know, give me the fire maker, Grace."

"It's called a lighter," she said, placing it in his upturned palm.

"Never mind what it's called. You won't use it again."

"So how am I supposed to get fires going then?"

"The same manner as I do," he said, handing her a flint.

"You have got to be joking?"

"I have never been more serious about anything. You will learn to use it."

"Can't I just use the lighter in the house?"

"No."

"That's crazy. I have a bag full of them and no one is going to see me using it in the house."

"Grace, I said, no. Once... that is all it will take, and you will be on a stake with a fire at your feet."

She drew a deep breath and straightening her shoulders turned toward the stairs.

"Right, well I guess I'll go and get a blanket then. OK to use the lamp I lit with the lighter?"

"Sarcasm isn't an attractive quality, Grace. You know perfectly well that I won't stop you using the lamp and you understand why I've taken the lighter off you. Stop sulking and behave like an adult."

A moment's thought told her he was right, told her that she was being childish and that he was only looking after her. But she had slipped the lighter into the pocket of her dress hoping to impress him, hoping to bring something of use to his life. Instead he had slapped her down like a naughty child. Humiliation, more than anger, burned in her face as she climbed the last step to the landing.

The rooms at the top of the stairs were familiar and her mood lightened a bit as she passed the door to what would be Harry's room, nearly four hundred years from now. Not much would change with the building over the years. Plasterboard would be added to smooth out the walls, a carpet here and there, but essentially the space would remain the same.

Still shivering, Grace found a pile of roughly woven blankets and wrapped one around her shoulders. It had been kind of Robert's sister to lend her the gown but it was no more suited to the bitter cold and heavy snow than her jeans and sweatshirt had been. She was going to need a coat if she were to have any chance of surviving the winter.

Back in the main room of the post house Grace warmed herself in front of the fire whilst Robert moved around the room lighting the oil lamps.

"Why is there no one staying in the rooms upstairs?"

"I closed up when I made the journey to Derbyshire two weeks ago."

"Are you expecting it to be busy today?"

"Yes. Every room in the city has been filled."

"Do you just leave the place at night then and go home?"

"No. I live here."

"Will you be living here tonight?"

"Yes and so will you."

"Where do we sleep then?"

He nodded to a door off the main building.

"Through there. Patrons are upstairs."

"Can I do anything to help?"

"No. I'm ready to open the doors now."

"Can I help once you open?"

"What is it you would like to do?"

"I don't know. Whatever you need help with. What about the rooms upstairs? Could I clean them up a bit?"

"If you wish, but Grace, you are not to use anything that doesn't belong in this time. If you are going to work you do it in the way of my time, not yours."

"Fine," she said, annoyed at him for making reference to the lighter again.

"There is fresh bedding in the room in which you found the blanket. I would be obliged if you would prepare the beds, but leave the fires."

"Why?"

"A waste of fuel and they are a hazard. Patrons pay for a bed, not warmth."

They both turned to the door as the sound of arriving trade gathered outside.

"Shall I get the doors?"

"No, I will do it."

"Right, well I'll go upstairs and sort the rooms out then," she said, leaving Robert to his customers.

Grace pulled herself upright, placing her hands in the small of her back. Making beds the old fashioned way was hard work and it had been a long time since she had put anything like this amount of physical effort into household chores. Having swept and dusted the rooms and made up the beds, Grace was happy with the results. She would have liked to have put some flowers in the rooms. But on further reflection she dismissed the idea, thinking that Robert was unlikely to approve.

Turning to leave, she gasped in surprise as she noticed a man lazily propped between the doorframes.

"Can I help you?"

"I thought the price was extortionate," he said, giving her a long hard stare, "but I don't so much mind the fee if there's a little extra on offer."

"Mr. Hamilton's prices are fair. There isn't a room to be had anywhere in the city," she said, defensively.

"As I said, I don't mind the fee... now," he replied, sauntering toward her.

Nervously she stepped backwards, positioning herself behind a chair.

"I need to be going now," she stammered.

He drew closer, his eyes wild and challenging. He kicked the chair to the side and grabbed at her. She stepped back into the bed frame. Trapped between him and the bed, she froze.

"Resisting?" he said, making another grab for her gown and pulling her hard against him. She fought him wildly, but his grip was too firm. He took a handful of her hair in his free hand and yanked her head backwards.

"I like them wild," he said, tugging harder on her hair.

Tears welled in her eyes as she tried to lift her foot to kick him, but the weight and sheer volume of the skirts made injuring the man unlikely.

"Please," she cried, "let go of me."

"Not likely," he said, hooking his right leg behind hers and pushing her backwards onto the bed.

The full weight of his body fell on top of her. She screamed and lifted her hands to his face, clawing her nails down the length of his cheek. He slapped her hard across her face. For a moment the room went black, her head swam and her ear rang from the force of the blow.

Suddenly, she could breath and the weight of his body was gone. Grace scrambled up to see the man hovering in mid air, his face white with shock. Robert's eyes blazed dangerously as he deposited the man on his feet. With one swift turn of his head, Robert smacked the edge of his forehead across the bridge of the man's nose.

The stranger dropped to the floor and within seconds was lying in a pool of his own blood. Robert grabbed him by the shirt and pulled him up. The man swayed unsteadily on his feet.

"No, Robert, leave him," Grace screamed. Scrambling off the bed she flung herself at Robert, begging him to stop.

"You'll kill him, Robert. Please, let him go?"

Robert stared at the man for a brief moment before flinging him aside.

"Get out!" he ordered, "Now!"

The dazed man staggered through the door leaving a trail of blood behind him.

"Are you alright?" he asked, looking across at Grace.

She shook fiercely and tears streaked her cheeks but she nodded her head.

"Stay here," he said, turning to leave the room.

Moments later he returned to find Grace curled up on the bed sobbing. He sat beside her, gently resting his hand on her shoulders.

"I am sorry," he whispered.

She tried to reply, to tell him it wasn't his fault, that she didn't blame him, but the words caught in her throat. She clung to him, sobbing like a child as he held her against him and soothed a lifetime's pain.

When finally the tears had stopped and her head pounded from the crying, she got to her feet.

"I'm sorry," she said, rubbing her forehead.

"Sorry for what? You haven't done anything wrong." He paused thoughtfully cupping his hands together. "Don't ever apologize to me again," he said, turning to leave. "We're going home."

"What about your customers?"

"There aren't any. I've closed the doors."

"Because of me?"

"No! For you."

"I don't understand," she said, quietly.

"This is no place for a lady."

"But this is your livelihood. You can't just close the doors."

"I can and I have."

"How will you live, Robert?"

"That is not your concern."

"Please, don't make me carry the guilt and worry that you will have no money because of me."

"This is my decision alone to make and not your burden to carry. However, I can assure you, Grace, that if this house never opens again, I will not starve and nor will you."

It all became too much for her; the loss of her daughter, the pain of her loveless marriage, the belief that she was mentally ill, the bizarre notion that she had travelled through time, his kindness and love, this new and terrifying world.

Tears welled in her eyes again, threatening to overspill. Her stomach lurched as if she was going to be sick and her hands shook uncontrollably. Confusion and pain surged inside her until the tears broke free and her body and mind felt numb to the world.

******

CHAPTER 8

He turned and walked toward the fireplace. She watched him as he rested in front of it and lowered a log gently into the flames. He reached for a thick cloth on the hearth and lifted a pot from above the fire. Cautiously, he poured boiling water from the pot into two mugs and returned the cast iron pot to the fire.

"I've grown quite fond of your coffee," he said, handing her a mug and moving to sit on the edge of the bed.

"Have you ever had coffee before?"

"Yes, but it tasted nothing like this."

"What did it taste like?"

"Bitter."

She blew gently across the rim of the mug. Steam circled off the liquid and threaded up into the cool air of the room.

"Robert in my time, your post house is owned by one of your brother's descendents."

He clasped his hands and pursed his lips thoughtfully. "I have seen him."

"I know, and he has seen you. His name is Harry."

"Harry?" he smiled broadly, "Well I know which brother he's from."

She cocked her head quizzically. "You do?"

"Yes, I do. It'll be Harry."

Grace smiled and a gentle laugh escaped her throat. "I didn't think to ask your brother's names."

"No reason why you should."

"So your sister is Sarah and your brother is Harry. But you have another brother?"

"I do, George."

"George?" Grace gasped wondering if it could be possible.

"That's what I said."

"In my time a George owns this house," Grace said with a grin.

They sat in a comfortable silence, sipping the warm drink. She closed her eyes and savored its flavor, wondering ruefully what life was going to be like without her jar of instant coffee. It seemed a bizarre thing to muse over and she sighed at her apparent shallowness. A gust of wind howled down the narrow street between the Minster and the house disturbing their calm. Robert moved toward the fire and added another log of wood to the glowing embers.

"Will I meet your family?"

"When you feel ready."

"What if they don't like me?"

She sounded truly anxious. He hadn't anticipated her reaction and it threw him momentarily.

"You care what my family thinks?"

"Of course I care. They're your family."

He weighed her words, considering carefully his own feelings on the subject. Would it matter to him if his family didn't accept her? Yes, he concluded, it would matter, but it mattered more what she thought of them.

He took a deep breath, contemplating the complexities that had become his life. A loyal servant to the king, he had fought as a Cavalier in the civil war, travelled the continent with his master and returned with the restoration. But in all that time he had never considered marriage.

Of course there had been women. Life with the king, even in exile, had included an almost constant trail of female characters of loose morals and flighty manners. They had come and gone with the movements of the entourage and never had one remained more than briefly in his memory.

Resting his elbows on his thighs and stretching his arms out in front of him he clasped his hands thoughtfully. His eyes stared at the flames as they danced and leapt around the brickwork of the fireplace. This was how it had all began, he thought. Idle eyes staring dimly at a flame, a blurred image materializing within the flame.

Had he the slightest belief in sorcery and magic he would almost certainly have killed this woman on sight. But he had never paid attention to the ramblings of the witch hunters. Magic was simply unexplained events and sorcery didn't exist.

He mused over the irony of his conviction. In his readiness to dismiss her as a master of evil magic he had allowed her to enchant him.

As if aware of his musings she shuffled across the bed. She sat cross legged beside him, her hand resting lightly on his thigh.

"Do people in the future move through time often?"

She looked startled. "No. Time travel isn't possible."

"Not impossible," he replied.

"No, I suppose not, but it's deemed to be."

"Yet you are here."

"I guess so."

"Do you believe in witches?"

"No, that's daft. Witches aren't real. They exist for the purpose of children's tales and adult fantasy. They are no more real than magic is."

"If magic is isn't real and witches are fantasy and time travel is impossible, how do you explain how you got here?"

His words hit her with the force of a physical blow. She stared at his face, the color draining from hers.

"I can't."

He watched her, his dark eyes blazed dangerously. She met his look and held it as fear ripped through her. His eyes demanded the truth but she had none to give.

"I know," he said, eventually. "There's no reason why I should trust you, but I do."

He got up from the bed and moved to close the shutter. The flame from a single candle glowed against the whitewashed wall behind her bedside table. She watched anxiously as he stoked the fire and the flames grew up around the fresh logs.

"Did you love your husband?" he asked, replacing the poker on its stand.

"I thought I did... once."

"And now?"

"No," she whispered quietly.

He lifted her backpack and handbag and set them on the bed beside her.

"Tomorrow we will go through this. These things must be destroyed."

"No, Robert you can't."

"I can and I will," he said, sternly. "If you are ever seen using any of these things you will face trial for witchcraft."

He was right and Grace understood the risks. But she had no intention of letting him destroy anything she had brought with her.

Fumbling with the zip she opened the backpack and emptied its content onto the bed.

He stood on the opposite side of the bed watching her as she reached for a small square box.

"See these?" she said, holding the box up for him to see.

He nodded silently.

"These are called painkillers. They do what their name suggests. They kill pain and fever. Robert, they save lives."

"Grace, you were not listening to me. The usefulness of these things is not in question. Your survival is."

"We can hide them. No one need ever know."

"And where would you have me hide these things?"

Flustered her eyes flicked frantically around the room, settling on the oak wardrobe that would remain in this room for nearly four hundred years.

"In the wardrobe," she said, excitedly.

A loud laugh bellowed from him, breaking the tension of the room.

"So, no one is going to find them in there?"

"No... No, they won't. Not if you add a false bottom to it."

He pursed his lips, pondered her suggestion for a few minutes.

"Alright, I'll do it," he said, suddenly.

"You will?"

"I will," he said, letting a broad smile cross his lips.

A soft glow from the embers of the fire lit the room. He reached out and touched her gently with his hand as she turned restlessly away from him. She rolled onto her back and her eyes sprang open. The beamed ceiling glared down on her. Her mind twisted and in fits of confusion, her heart pounded and her stomach churned.

"I saw her," she whispered.

"Saw who?"

"Jenny."

"Your daughter?"

She sat bolt upright, her hand fumbling for the photograph on her bedside table.

"Yes," she breathed, clutching the picture to her breast, "my daughter."

"Tell me what happened?"

She stared at him blankly, her mind fighting to recover the dying images of her dream.

"She's in trouble."

"What sort of trouble?"

"I don't know."

A knot of fear tightened in her stomach as she replayed the dying moments of her dream to him.

"Jenny was screaming; a desperate terrified cry for help. I tried to get to her but I couldn't."

"Where was she?"

"I don't know... but it felt like... I was in water and... the closer I got to her, the thicker the water became until I couldn't pull myself through the water anymore... And I woke up."

"It was only a dream, Grace."

"No, it was more than a dream. Jenny needs me and I don't know how to help her."

In desperation she sprung out of bed and grabbed her cell phone. She flicked madly through her the address book looking for Jenny's number.

"I know what to do," she said, suddenly staring at the cell. "I need the portrait."

He came to stand in front of her, his arms moving to encircle her waist. She slipped from his embrace and ran to the fireplace. She turned to him, her eyes pleading.

"I can't reach it."

In one stride he was beside her, his arms stretched toward the portrait.

"Grace, sit down and we will talk about this," he said, handing the frame to her.

She shook her head frantically, taking the frame from him.

"No, there's no time," she replied, dropping to the floor. "Robert, pass me the backpack, please?"

He did as she asked and then slid to the floor beside her. He watched her as she ripped the bag open and scrambled through its contents.

"What are you looking for?"

"The pens, Robert, I'm looking for my bloody ballpoint pens. Have you got a desk?"

"I have. Why?"

"Cut the legs off it. Now," she demanded.

"What?"

"You heard me, get the damn legs off it."

"Grace, this is enough. Stop."

"I can't, Robert, there isn't much time. It might be too late already."

"Alright, I'll cut the legs off the desk but you are going to tell me what is going on first."

Blind with panic she grabbed a pen but he caught her hand and held it steady.

"Grace, tell me what you are doing."

"Just let me go, please," she said, struggling to extract her hand from his.

He shook his head seriously. "Not until you tell me what you are doing. Now give me the pen and start at the beginning."

Her hand trembled as she released the pen.

"Thank you," he said, setting the pen on the floor beside him. "Now tell me what you were going to write and to whom?"

"A letter, Robert, I need to write a letter to myself."

"And how is this going to help Jenny?"

"Well it won't directly help her but it will lead to something that will help her," she said, falling over her words as she raced to finish the explanation.

"I'm not following you, Grace. Start at the beginning, please."

With much reluctance she told him about the letter she had found on the back of the portrait in her hotel room and how his desk had come to belong to Kate because she had fallen in love with the idea that Robert had commissioned the making of the desk specifically for her.

"If you don't make that desk appear to have been made for me then Kate will not buy it and the future will be altered. I was meant to come here. I see that now but I also know that we must not change what should happen in my time. You must write a note with the exact measurements of your desk and it must appear as though you had it made for your wife.

He smiled a broad slightly cheeky smile and she shot him a look of disapproval.

"What are you smiling about? This isn't funny."

"I know it's not funny, but you have twice answered a question you said you should not."

"What?"

"You will be my wife?"

She clapped her hand hard over her mouth realizing with horror what she had done.

He moved her hand slowly from her mouth and gently kissed her lips.

"You haven't changed anything. I knew from the first moment I saw you that you would be my wife."

Her head spun in an ever tighter vortex of confusion, the only coherent thought being that she needed to help her daughter.

"You are right and I'm sorry but I can't think about it now. I have to help Jenny."

He nodded, handing the pen back to her. She took it from him and began to write, her hand darting furiously across the canvass. When she was done he placed the portrait back on the wall above the fireplace.

"Is that it?"

"No, please pass me my cell?"

One dark brow quirked in question.

"That... thing over there on the bed."

She took the cell off him and ran her fingers over the touch screen, then lifted it to her mouth and began to speak.

"Harry, this is Grace and I need your help. My daughter is in trouble. Please, Harry, you've got to find her? She lives at The Vicarage, 114 Monnies End, Clowne, Derbyshire and her name is Jenny.

"The details for my bank account are in my hotel room. Use the money as you see fit. When you find Jenny, please give her this cross. She will know it is from me and understand its significance," Grace paused and tapped the cell against her top lip. "Harry, tell her that I love her."

Grace lifted her hands to the back of her neck and unclipped the chain. She watched it as it dropped neatly into the palm of her hand.

"Robert do you have a metal box?"

"I do," he said, disappearing from the room, to return a few minutes later. He laid the box on the floor in front of her, along with a small leather pouch. She looked up at him quizzically.

"What's this?"

"Just a little something to help my future nephew through life."

Grace gently untied the leather thongs and pulled the pouch open. She gaped in amazement at the shining gold coins.

"Robert there's a fortune here."

"Only a small one, assuming gold still has a value in your time."

"Oh yes, gold still has a value in my time," she said, weighing the heavy coins in the palm of her hand.

"I take it you have a way of getting this... cell to Harry?"

Grace opened the lid of the metal box and placed the cell phone, the silver cross and the leather pouch into the box.

"I do," she said, routing through the backpack again.

"What are you looking for now?"

"My purse. Jenny will need my bank card to get access to the funds in my account."

"If you have no idea how you moved nearly four hundred years in time, how are you going to move this box?" he asked, frowning down on her.

"Yes, that is easier than it sounds. We need to go back to the post house."

"The post house?"

"Yup."

"Not now, surely?" he said, casting a disapproving eye at her.

She nodded solemnly. "Yes, please?"

"Grace it's the dead of night. The snow is knee deep and still falling and you have no coat. Can't this wait until the morning?"

"No, Robert it really can't. I will go on my own if I have to, but this has to be done now."

A low guttural groan emanated from his throat as he pulled a cotton shirt over his head.

"It won't take long, I promise," she said, wrestling herself into the borrowed gown.

"Exactly why does it have to be the post house?"

"Because in the letter I have just written on the back of your portrait I told myself to tell Harry to look under the floorboards in the post house."

"I see," he said, as understanding started to take hold. "You are putting these things somewhere for Harry to find in the future."

She nodded excitedly. "That's exactly what I'm doing."

"Couldn't you have told Harry to look under the floorboards in this house?"

"No, because I've already given him the message."

"I see. We'd better go then," he said, handing her an oversized black coat.

"I can't take your coat."

"You can and you will. I have another one," he said, as they made their way through the main living room downstairs.

"Robert, wait," she said, opening a cabinet and removing a glass bottle.

"From what you've said, Harry can do without any more whisky," he said, stopping beside her.

Grace pulled the cork from the neck of the bottle.

"It's not for Harry," she said, lifting the whisky to her mouth and drinking deeply from the bottle.

"Steady, girl," he said, lifting his hand to take the bottle from her.

She gasped and shuddered as the liquid slid down the back of her throat.

"It was for me," she finished.

"Yes, I can see that."

"Funny," she said, smiling gently to herself.

"What's funny?"

"Harry used to call me, girl," she said, hooking her arms into the long black coat.

Robert chuckled to himself as he watched her move clumsily toward the door. The coat hung heavily around her shoulders, her arms lost in the sleeves and her small frame drowned by the thick cloth.

"You look ridiculous," he said, trying to suppress a laugh.

She shot him an angry look but it did nothing to suppress the laughter building inside him. Unable to help himself he put his arms out and drew her into an affectionate hug.

"I shouldn't have laughed at you. I'm sorry," he said, trying to sound serious.

"Let's just go," Grace snapped back.

They made their way through the darkened city. The snow still lay deep underfoot and Grace struggled with the added weight of the coat on top of her dress, but she was grateful for its addition nonetheless. The night air was bitter. Her eyes watered and her cheeks stung, but the only thought she had was for her daughter.

Robert slid the key into the lock and turned it. The door pushed silently open into the main room of the posting house. They fumbled their way toward the bar, looking for an oil lamp. Grace stared in shocked silence as Robert flicked the lighter and brought the flame to the wick of a lamp. The light guided them to the small room off what would be the kitchen. Robert placed the lamp on an oak table and looked curiously at the floor.

"How can you be sure no one will find this before Harry does?"

"I can't," she said, simply.

"So you don't know for sure that he is going to get this?"

"No. I left him before he lifted the floorboards," she paused thoughtfully, "I'm not sure what would have happened if I'd stayed. On one hand, I would have known for sure that the box was still there. On the other hand... I would probably have headed straight back to Jack had I known Jenny was in trouble."

He frowned curiously at her. "Tell me, Grace. Your cell, could it exist in two times?"

"I don't think so... at least I can't see how it could."

"So perhaps it is a good thing you didn't stay and watch Harry lift the boards."

"Perhaps, but now I will never know if Harry will get this box."

"Yes, you will."

"How?"

"We leave nothing under these floorboards."

"That's a great idea," she said, sardonically, "Absolutely bloody great. So I get to know for sure that Harry never finds anything there."

"That's right."

"And how exactly is that meant to help Jenny," she snapped.

"We're going back to the house."

"No, Robert, we can't. I've got to get this message to Harry."

"We will."

"But he is expecting it to be here."

"Am I right in saying that it doesn't matter where he finds it?"

"Well... I guess it doesn't matter, just so long as he gets it. But, he won't know to look anywhere else for it."

"He doesn't have to."

"You aren't making any sense, Robert and we're wasting time. Please, just help me lift the floorboards?"

"No, we're not lifting anything. Trust me, Grace. Harry will get your message."

"I don't have much choice, do I?"

"No, you don't," he said, with all seriousness.

They made the walk back to the house in silence. Dawn was breaking and the city rose around them. Grace pushed the heavy weave of the coat aside and gathered the sodden skirts of her gown in her hands in an attempt to speed up their journey but progress was still slow. Robert walked steadily beside her, matching her pace. It made her think of Jack and how he would charge off ahead of her and Jenny whenever they were out together. He believed it was the woman's place to walk behind her husband. In truth the man had walked so fast that the two of them had often found themselves running behind him in their attempt to keep up. Yet here was a man, who should see her as inferior, yet he chose to walk steadily beside her.

Robert's heart broke for the woman beside him. He understood her pain and was wise enough to know that there was little he could do to ease it. Time, he assumed would be the most efficient healer. But he doubted she would ever recover fully from the loss of her daughter. His fists clenched at the thought of the man who had forced her to leave her daughter. They were common enough; weak in nature and bullies at heart, he despised such characters. But for now there was the more pressing issue of her daughter. He was fairly confident he had devised a plan that would ensure the timely delivery of Grace's message.

An orange glow stretched across the city as the stars faded and dawn broke clear and crisp. Robert pushed the door to the house open and ushered Grace hurriedly inside. She slithered clumsily out of the coat, her shoulders straightening as its weight disappeared. Her skirts hung limp and muddy around her ankles as she moved closer to the fire in an attempt to dry the sodden material.

"You are too close to the fire, Grace," he said, pulling her gently back from the flames.

"Go upstairs and put your old clothes on," he said.

"I thought you said I wasn't to wear them again?"

"I did."

Too tired to argue she nodded and made her way wearily up the stairs to the bedroom. She found her jeans and sweatshirt neatly folded in the chest. The photograph of Jenny lay on the rug beside the backpack, forgotten in the earlier panic. Unable to help herself, her eyes fixed on the picture. Although the image tore savagely at her heart, her body and mind were too exhausted to muster even a sob. Clutching the photograph of her daughter she made her way down the stairs in search of Robert.

Shelves of leather bound books lined the walls of the room in which Grace found him. The metal box sat open on a desk which she recognized instantly. He smiled up at her as she entered the room.

"Warmer now?" he asked as she came to stand beside the desk.

"Yes, thank you," she said, softly holding her hands out to the flames of the fire, "What are you going to do?"

His finger rested on a piece of paper which he slid across the desk toward her. Her eyes scanned the familiar words.

'To be of the finest quality with exact dimension to ensure the absolute comfort of my dearest wife.'

"Is there anything you would like to say to Kate?" he said, lifting the quill and dipping it lightly in the ink well.

"I don't understand," she said, watching his hand as it carefully crafted letters on a sheet of paper. Intent on the words he was writing, Robert didn't answer. Finally when he had finished writing he turned the page to her.

Dear Kate,

This is Robert Hamilton. I hope you don't mind the intrusion and please forgive me for any inconvenience this desk or I may have caused you. I write to you in urgency about a matter of extreme importance regarding Grace's daughter, Jenny. Enclosed with this letter is Grace's cell. May I be so bold as to request that you deliver this item to Harry Hamilton without delay, along with one of the two leather pouches? The remaining pouch is for you, in compensation for any trouble this desk and I may have caused you.

Yours most sincerely
Robert and Grace Hamilton

Grace stared wide eyed up at him.

"It's brilliant," she whispered.

He lifted the note off the table, folded it in half and placed it neatly in the box.

"No, wait," she cried as he was about to close the lid. "Pass me the cell?"

"What's wrong?"

"The battery, I need to take it out of the cell or it won't work in four hundred years time."

He raised his brow in question but didn't voice it. That, he thought could wait for another day.

Robert watched as she slid a sheet off the back of the cell. He noticed the slight tremble of her hands and resisted the urge to help her. He had no understanding of her world and reasoned that there was little he could do to help. Clipping a finger nail into the device she levered what appeared to be a thin metal block out of the cell and dropped it onto the desk. He assumed this must be the battery.

She laid the cell in the box, without the battery, and slowly closed the lid.

"It's ready," she said, resting her hand protectively on the cold lid of the box.

"Do you need to make a false bottom for the drawer?"

"No."

"But I told Kate there was a false bottom to the drawer. She won't find the box," she said, starting to panic.

"She will find it Grace. There is already a false bottom to this drawer."

He watched her visibly relax as he lowered the box into its hiding place. It seemed almost incomprehensible that this box would remain undisturbed, for nearly four hundred years. He prayed a silent prayer that it would be found in tact by Kate and provides the help Jenny needed.

"Thank you," she whispered, as he pushed the drawer closed.

"My pleasure."

"Robert, we've forgotten the legs of the desk?"

"No, we haven't."

"We have. In the future the desk appears shorter and smaller."

He smiled knowingly down at her.

"That won't be a problem," he said, starting to clear the desk of its content.

"Do you have a saw?"

"I don't need one, Grace. This desk was made when I was in exile with the king. It was designed to come apart for easy transportation. The legs are in two parts and the pedestals slide apart."

Within minutes Robert had altered the desk to a smaller, shorter piece of furniture. Grace stared, mouth open at it.

"All those years the world believed you had this made for your wife and it was just a piece of furniture you carried around Europe," she said, not bothering to hide the disappointment in her voice.

He bent and kissed her lightly on the cheek before dropping on one knee in front of her. He took her hand gently in his and trailed his lips over each finger.

"My dear Grace," he said, taking her left hand in his, "would you do me the honor of becoming my wife?"

She stared down at him in shock.

"But I'm already... married," she whispered.

"Not in this time you are not."

She considered her marriage vows to Jack. She had pledged her life to him in front of God. But then hadn't she broken that pledge the day she left him? Was the act of divorce the sin, or was it remarriage that God condemned? She had already committed the gravest of sins by sharing Robert's bed. Did this mean that she was doomed to an eternity of hell? Her mind whirled in an ever more confused jumble of thoughts. She had broken every oath she had ever made, and now she feared the wrath of God.

Grace dropped her head and met his look. She could see the reflection of her face and the light of the fire in his eyes. She loved this man like she had loved no other. Their souls were bound beyond time. She was meant to be with him. Was it not God who had sent her to his side?

He watched her face as it broke from a look of terror into a beautiful and radiant smile.

"Robert Hamilton, nothing would give me greater pleasure than to become your wife."

"In which case," he said, slipping a simple gold band onto her left hand, "may I be so bold as to offer you a desk, customized for you... as a small token of my undying love."

THE END

How are Grace and Robert connected to Simon and Corran of 'When Fate Dictates'?
I'd love to tell you, but that would ruin the surprise…
Find out in 'Entwined', book three of the Highland Secret Series.
To give you some clues, here follows an excerpt from 'Entwined'.

ENTWINED

York- 16th December, Modern Day

Kate slid her thumb over the tracker pad, watching as the blue strip highlighted her friends' names one after the other. She lifted her thumb off the pad as the strip hovered over Grace's name. For the past few hours she had been repeatedly dialing the number, but each time the call had gone straight to Grace's answer phone.

Dropping the cell on the duvet, she slid off the bed and reached for her leggings and jumper. The iPod docking station on the bedside table told her it was three o'clock in the morning - four hours since Grace had left. It was too late to call the hotel she was staying at, and she couldn't call the police until she was sure Grace was missing.

Kate shivered as the wind howled past her house. She pulled the curtain aside and stared into the orange glow of the street light, mesmerized by frantic flakes of snow as they whipped around its outer glass cover. Her fears were totally justified. Grace had promised to call her when she got back to the hotel and she hadn't. Cursing for not insisting that her friend catch a taxi home, Kate grabbed her beanie and gloves and made her way downstairs.

She struggled to stand as the wind pounded her unmercifully. She ducked her head against the icy blast, gasping a quick breath before facing the oncoming wind again. Deep banks of snow rose up the side of buildings narrowing her passage to an almost impassable gap between the drifts. Blindly she stumbled through the city hoping with every trudging step that her friend was tucked up in bed, dreaming of her haunting Cavalier. Exhausted, Kate sought shelter in the recess of a doorway. Her leggings clung to her calves like frozen limpets and her legs burnt painfully now that she had stopped moving. Lifting her fingers to her mouth, she caught the woolen tip in her teeth and pulled the sodden glove from her hand. She watched the sign of the Cavalier Hotel swaying in the wind. She raised her head to the window of her friend's, room. Her look fixed intently on the panes of glass, but the glazed section of the window offered her no reassuring sight. Her eyes streamed with tears as the lashing wind stung her face. A wave of impending doom washed over her as she left the shelter of the doorway and plunged once again into the open street. A curtain of snow fell steadily before her in a never-ending stream of white. Kate lost her footing and stumbled, steadying herself against the base of a streetlight. Her breathing was shallow and painful, her mind clouded and confused. Her legs felt unsteady and weak as tiredness crept into every muscle and bone of her body. She closed her eyes against the pounding wind and rested her head heavily against the icy pole. Through the whirl of confusion, Kate understood that she had to find shelter. Willing her body and mind from its stupor, she took one deep, burning breath and dragged herself from the pole. She swayed unsteadily on her feet but remained upright enough to stagger her way down Stonegate. With reason and direction long since lost, instinct drove her to Harry's pub where, finally, overcome with exhaustion, she collapsed heavily in the deserted courtyard.

Unable to sleep and painfully aware of the conversation that day break would bring, Harry slid out of bed and walked slowly to the window. His fingers drew the curtains aside and then tensed on the cloth. He blinked in an attempt to focus his eyes, certain he had caught a glimpse of something moving in the shadows of the courtyard. Cursing, he let the curtain fall and reached for his coat.

"Simon..."

******

ABOUT THE AUTHOR

Elizabeth Marshall is the writing alter ego of a lady born in St Mary's Hospital, at the Marianhill Monastery, in the province of Natal, South Africa and was brought up in a small, rural Natal village surrounded by a large Scottish farming family.

Her primary education was delivered by Nuns from the monastery in which she was born. Through secondary school into adulthood, Elizabeth's life centered on a love of music, reading, writing and history.

After Elizabeth married she settled in the UK with her husband. She has worked at the Charing Cross and Westminster Medical School in England, Nottingham Social Services in England and is currently a Director of an IT Project Management Consultancy.

Elizabeth lives in the city of York, England with her husband and children. She spends her spare time with her head in a book or her fingers on the keyboard writing one.

'When Fate Dictates' is book one in
the 'Highland Secret' series.
Book two of the series is called 'Beyond Time'
and book three is 'Entwined'.

Find Elizabeth Marshall online.
Email: Elizabeth@elizabethmarshallwrites.com
Website: www.elizabethmarshallwrites.com/
Twitter: twitter.com/@em_writes
Facebook: www.facebook.com/emwrites
Amazon Author Page: amazon.com/author/elizabethmarshall

******

Printed in Great Britain
by Amazon.co.uk, Ltd.,
Marston Gate.